Home to Stay

CALLIE JAMES

ISBN: 0-9903646-3-1
ISBN-13: 978-0-9903646-3-4

This story is a work of fiction and
a creation of the author's imagination.

DEDICATION

For Mom

Thank you for all of your love and support. I truly would not have made it through some of those *new mom* years without you.

I've been planning this dedication since I finished writing my first romance novel twenty-plus years ago. I wasn't quite a teenager when you handed me my first sweet romance, Mom, and I haven't been the same since. Clearly, the genre made an impact. Thank you for inadvertently pointing me down a path that would lead me to such a fulfilling and creative outlet that I love with all my heart.

CONTENTS

CALLIE JAMES

ACKNOWLEDGMENTS

My deepest thanks to my beta readers and copy editors for all their hard work. Dave, Kris and Carol…you kept me sane.

CHAPTER ONE

"Hey, Jess."

Jessie Brewer would have loved a phone call or text message. *Some* kind of warning he was back in town. At least she would have been prepared when she opened her door tonight to find him—one of America's most eager heroes and best-kept secrets—looking deservedly sheepish and standing in the pouring rain like a desperate man.

He didn't offer an explanation but gave her a quick nod under the brim of his soaked, black Stetson. When that rare half-grin appeared, for the briefest moment, she wondered if she'd finally cracked from all those years of chaos and stress. But she centered quickly and clutched the doorframe, watching those gorgeous dimples deepen as her heart hammered a wary thump-thump. Clearly, he thought those baby blues and disarming grin might warrant an invitation into the house. When she didn't react beyond a questioning frown, he took a small step forward, barely under the shelter of the porch roof now and almost within touching distance as his large six-foot-three frame caused one of her flimsy porch boards to creak under his weight. Technically, one of *their* flimsy porch boards.

His hat dipped as his attention shifted down over her

cleaning garb. She followed his gaze to the worn, baggy jeans sporting a large hole in the knee and cinched at the waist with a thick belt. The large, open flannel covered her black tank top, hiding her most recent, dramatic weight loss. She chanced a glance at him, noticing that his focus *did* rest on her waist a little too long before moving to one of her yellow, rubber gloves and the old, wet t-shirt balled in her hand.

His wet t-shirt.

A frown pulled at his mouth, showing deep lines that emphasized his tired features as his dark gaze settled on her face again. "You've lost weight."

The concern in his eyes had almost softened her heart. Until he'd said *that*. "Tell me you're not here to talk about my weight." Weariness had laced her words, even as she'd tried to keep her voice level. No surprise. She'd never been able to pull it together around him. Apparently, a divorce from Matthew Brewer and a full year away from him hadn't changed that fact. "Brody isn't here, Matt. What do you want?"

"I'm not here to see our son. At least not yet," he added, pinching the brim of his hat as the wind picked up. "I'm here to see you."

She frowned. Certainly a phone call would have sufficed.

"I realize I could have called." Thunder cracked as another wave of heavy rain blew in on a violent, swirling gust, pelting his Stetson loudly in the back and showering his neck in rivulets. He barely seemed to notice, keeping his gaze fixed on her face. "But I figured you'd use every excuse in the book to avoid talking to me."

"No book needed." She held the dripping rag a bit higher for emphasis. "I'm in the middle of cleaning and I want to finish before… look, can't this wait?"

"It's important, Jess." He took a step closer and placed a hand against the doorframe, his thumb an inch from hers.

The porch light illuminated his square jaw under the brim of his hat, creating shadows that accented the strained lines bracketing his mouth. He was standing much too close; the tension rolling off him was palpable. He was probably waiting for her to shut the door in his face. It wouldn't be a first. Still, he looked determined. Matt was no bully, but she recognized the set in his jaw. He didn't plan to leave until she let him say whatever he'd come to say.

Looking at him tonight, she would have guessed him older than his thirty-two years. Without his amazing smile that transformed his features, it seemed the pressure of his unconventional job had finally taken a toll. Fatigue and worry had aged him ten years since she'd seen him last.

She wanted desperately to close the door, but pity and something else she couldn't name guided her hand to open it wider. With an unsteady breath, she took a step back and gestured with the wet rag for him to come in, and yes, please disrupt their lives once more.

His head tilted, one eyebrow arching at her welcome. When that half-grin followed, she whirled and hurried to the bucket she'd left on the kitchen tile, dropping his shirt into the soapy water. His larger-than-life presence filled the room behind her as she listened to his boots stepping from the front rug onto the hardwood floor. He shut the door quietly behind him, muting the rainstorm as he closed them in together.

"Where's Brody?" A combination of his low baritone and the high ceiling gave his question an echoing quality in the foyer, making him sound too close. She turned to find him still by the door, removing his Stetson. He dropped his hat onto the small table, covering her car keys and dousing any notion she had of escaping when this conversation took the usual turn for the worse.

The scruff on his jaw often meant he was too tired to care about his appearance. At least he looked tired. That light spattering of silver at his temples certainly hadn't

3

been there a year ago. His otherwise black, short hair remained a constant reminder of his earlier military service and the current profession he could rarely talk about, even to her when they were married.

"He's out with a friend," she said, pulling in a breath to steady her nerves. "I don't expect him back for a while." His gaze dropped to her waist again. Back up. She tried for a change of subject. "Are you staying with your folks?"

He nodded, confirming what she already knew, given he always stayed with his parents when in town since the divorce. Matt's parents were getting older, and maintaining a dude ranch and eighty-some horses took a great deal of work. His youngest sister and brother had stayed on as ranch employees and assisted with the foster children his parents took in from time to time. Matt helped when he came home to visit, and during those usually brief stays, Brody practically lived with them.

"How are they?" she said, trying to keep the conversation neutral. "Busy with holiday decorations, no doubt."

"I stopped here first, actually," he said, glancing around the foyer. "But I'm sure you're right. Pop probably put up the holiday decorations weeks ago." He turned his lingering gaze to the empty living room, which didn't yet boast so much as a snow globe.

"You stopped here first," she repeated, wringing her gloved hands. "I guess this really is important."

His attention pivoted to her gloves, that questioning frown deepening. "Mother mentioned in a voicemail that you don't come around much these days. They're both very worried about you."

She clenched her jaw, self-preservation making her pause. If she wanted to get rid of him, she knew she should keep her mouth shut. Just pretend the gossip didn't bother her. Maybe even say something genuine and nice. If only it were that easy. "They see Brody practically every day, Matt. In fact, I sometimes think he spends more time at the ranch than home. Your mother is being dramatic."

"They're not worried about Brody, Jess," he said, ignoring the pointed comment about his mother. "They're worried about *you*."

She opened her mouth but quickly reined in what likely would have been another defensive remark. Having grown accustomed to the talk around town ages ago, she still found it difficult not to get irritated when she learned yet again that she'd been the topic of someone's conversation. Small or large, Southern towns were funny that way, and given Brody's numerous issues, the gossip had become incessant. Truth be told, she loved Matt's parents. They were sincere in their concern, although their constant worry did nothing to curtail the talk that circulated. They had been good to her—well, mostly—and she was grateful for their love and support. But it wasn't always easy to like them. Rather, it wasn't always easy to like Matt's mother, whose constant *concern* could break a person for life.

"You're not denying it then," he said when she didn't respond. "My mother said that you've become a hermit. I figured she was exaggerating."

Fiona Brewer—Violet Valley's busiest busybody with all the best intentions, God bless her, *did* have a propensity for embellishment. Jessie pulled the yellow gloves from her hands and placed them on the counter while thinking through her answer. "I wouldn't say I'm a hermit. But between work and Brody, I don't exactly have oodles of extra time."

"Is that all?"

She turned to him. "Do you think I'm lying to you?"

"No," he said, his voice even. "I know that Luke picks up Brody every afternoon to help him with the horses and that he drops him off around six before you get home. My mother also mentioned you're working close to twelve-hour days again."

"It would seem your mother mentions quite a bit in her voicemails."

He shrugged. "Luke said something to her about it. He's worried about you, too."

"So have you talked to Luke yourself or is this all coming from her?"

"Luke and I spoke a couple of months ago, before the last job." Matt's profession left him out of pocket for weeks, sometimes months due to blackout periods when he couldn't communicate outside of his assignment.

"Well, all I ask is that you talk to him directly before making any judgments."

"No judgments, Jess," he said with a sigh. "It's as I said. She's only concerned."

"Yet somehow I feel she made it sound as though I'm off shopping instead of being a mother. Listen, Matt…Luke kindly offered to take Brody as a favor to me. To keep him socializing and out of trouble while I'm at work. That's all."

"I wasn't thinking anything else, Jess. I'm just talking here." His gaze softened as his focus dropped to her waist again. "So you're okay then?"

The genuine concern in his voice took her aback but she met his doubting gaze. "Of course." She turned abruptly. "I'm not saying it hasn't been busier at the shop since I took over," she said, crossing the living room to organize a bookshelf. "And I realize other moms can drive their kids to a million extracurricular activities and still make homemade cupcakes for the Sunday church bake sale, but I have a business to run now. I can't make it to the ranch for weekend dinners like I used to." She turned to him. "But you're welcome to take Brody whenever you'd like. You know…until you leave again."

He remained silent as a muscle tensed in his jaw. It annoyed her that she'd never been able to discern that granite expression of his. After knowing him most of her life, she should be able to read him better.

"About that. It's part of what I wanted to talk to you about tonight," he said.

His uncharacteristic hesitation caused her heartbeat to pulse in rapid succession. "*Which* part?"

"I'm going to be in town for a while."

"Hm." She forced her expression to remain neutral. "Brody didn't mention it."

"I haven't told him."

Taking a normal breath suddenly felt difficult, but she managed to pretend her growing panic wasn't about to choke her. She even smiled. "How long this time?" Christmas loomed just two weeks away. "After Christmas? New Year's?"

"A bit longer." He shifted his weight. "I've taken some time off."

"Hm." She grabbed her elbows and bit down on her lip, her mind racing at the idea of Matt in town for more than a few weeks.

"What?"

She realized she was chewing her lip and stopped. "You usually don't take time off unless you have to. Is something going on at the ranch?"

That half-grin appeared. "Something's *always* going on at the ranch. But that's not why I'm home. Just personal matters I need to attend to."

Personal matters? What personal matters? "What are we talking here? A month? Two? Three?"

"Possibly indefinitely."

The air felt too thin to breathe and her next question came out in a stutter. "In-indefinitely?"

"Probably."

"Well which is it? Possibly or probably?"

"Probably."

She braced her hand against the bookshelf to tamp down the panic hitting her full force now.

"Jess...I'm retiring," he finally said. "It's time, don't you think?"

Time? It was beyond time. Hell and gone beyond time. Two years ago, this move might have been a good thing. It might have even saved their marriage. Surely, he knew that. How could he do this to her now? Because *now* Matt returning home would disrupt everything. *Everything.* "But Brody is doing so well."

"Brody is doing so well?" he said. "What's that supposed to mean?"

"Um—" She shrugged. The statement had come across thoughtless, if not a little cruel, but what else could she say? Did he really plan to come back now, after she'd finally managed to get their lives in some type of order?

"I'm a little confused," he said, frowning. "You've asked me to quit every year for twelve years because Brody needs me here. *Your* words. Now suddenly he doesn't need me?"

Her thoughts zigzagged in a dozen directions. This was what she'd wanted for over a decade. Matt. Home safe. But why come home *now?* After all of this time. After years of trying and arguing and trying again. After a divorce that had nearly killed her. And after all of that, after she'd finally come to terms with this new reality—a life without Matt Brewer—he was back for good?

"Jessie?"

She looked up, the vision of him blurring through a welling of unshed tears. *Tears?* She turned from him and blinked repeatedly, swiping at her watering eyes and hoping he hadn't seen. "You're soaked," she said, her voice clogged with emotion as she motioned toward the master bedroom with a shaky hand. If she could get a moment, a full minute without him in the room, she could pull herself together. "I still have some of your things here. Maybe you should change your shirt before you catch your death." How ridiculous. Five minutes in the man's presence and she was already a mess of nerves.

"I want to talk about this," he said.

"We will." She sniffed, sounding like she had a head cold.

"You'll wait then?"

"Yes," she said, clearing her throat. "I'll wait."

"Thanks. I'll only be a minute."

She listened to his footsteps as he left the foyer before turning to see him weave his way through the living room with familiarity, until he disappeared down the hall that would lead to the bedroom.

Their bedroom.

The impact of a permanent return home, however unlikely, sank in quickly. Dread collided with crippling relief, and she stumbled to the small dining room table, sinking onto a hard chair. He'd be safe. Home and *safe*.

Finally.

She tried to blink back a decade of tears and worry, but it was useless. She sagged against the chair's back. Realized her limbs were shaking. She sniffled and shoved her head into her hands. She had a new life now. A safe life. One that didn't include Matt Brewer. She loved her responsibilities as new owner of the shop. And the new schooling arrangement with her son. And if she were to believe what Cole McLeod declared to her only last weekend, she had a new love in her life as well.

How could Matt do this to her now? The man hadn't been back ten minutes and he'd already twisted her life into a knot.

Once upon a time, she'd been a rational human being. In her head, everything made sense. She knew the mistakes she'd made in her marriage. She had a good idea where Matt had gone wrong. But every time she'd tried to fix it, every time *he'd* tried to fix it, they'd made things worse.

Until there had been nothing left to save.

Their marriage had been different in the beginning. The memory of that deep love still stole her breath if she allowed herself to think about it. They'd had so many plans. College. Careers. Three or four kids when they were financially ready. It should have all come together perfectly. But an early pregnancy had brought those plans to a screeching halt. With only two years of college, neither had been qualified to do anything beyond their fulltime day jobs. Working at his family's ranch hadn't paid Matt much, and her retail job at the shop had paid less. Combined, their incomes had barely covered their small mortgage, utilities, and food, much less school loans and daycare costs.

Brody had been good news for about five minutes, and then reality had hit them head-on. They'd put their plans on hold, Matt had joined the service, and their lives had changed irrevocably.

It had taken her thirteen years and a painful divorce to get some normal back into her life. Over the last year, she'd finally learned to breathe again, and now her ex-husband had come back to dismantle the quiet existence she'd worked so hard to create.

But why now? What was his motive?

She gripped her head tightly as each overwhelming thought ran through her mind. Maybe Matt's plan was to place Brody back in public school. Or maybe he'd heard that Cole was spending time with Brody and he didn't like the idea of his son having another male role model in his life.

Or worse, maybe Matt had returned for custody of his son.

*****

Standing in the master bath, Matt peeled the soaked shirt over his head as Terri's final words from a month-old voicemail replayed in his mind.

I'm telling you this because I'm her friend, Matt. Jessie isn't well and she needs you. Your son needs you. If you ever cared about Jessie at all, you'll swallow your pride, come back to Violet Valley this instant, and talk to her. Time to cowboy up.

Jessie needed him. He wouldn't have believed it had his ex-wife's best friend not said the words with such fierce intensity that she'd given him pause. He'd scarcely allowed himself to consider it before that day, had doubted it ever since, but when Jessie opened the door tonight to find him standing on the porch, he realized maybe Terri had been right. For several seconds, Jessie's guard had been down and to see her face…

That beautiful face had displayed a kaleidoscope of emotion. Surprise. Relief. The slightest of smiles. Then, of course, utter disappointment when she realized they might actually have to talk.

Scowling, he turned and grabbed a towel from the closet, rubbing it hard over his arms and torso. Making her cry only five minutes into a conversation had to be a record. Her tears had surprised him, probably because he hadn't seen much in over four years that indicated she cared. Not that he could talk in that department. How had they even hit this point? The arguments. The divorce. The years had moved so quickly, yet the memories of those blowouts were always right there. When he thought of home, he thought of arguing with Jessie, or worse, the unbearable silence that always followed.

It would help matters if he had some idea where to go from here. Terri's voice had sounded desperate when she'd called him and he'd thought of little else than getting back to Violet Valley as soon as possible. Now standing in their house—*her* house—he was at a complete loss. Truth be told, he didn't trust this wouldn't end up in another fight.

Leaning forward, he braced his elbows against the pale countertop. That first meeting could have gone better. *You've lost weight.* Really genius? Nice icebreaker.

But seeing her again had been a shock. A big one. The last time they'd been face-to-face, her dark brown hair had been long, thick and wavy. He remembered distinctly how she'd curled it around her finger, looking nervous as he'd hugged Brody goodbye and left for good. Sometime over the last year she'd layered and straightened it, which emphasized her heart-shaped face and oval eyes. When she opened the door tonight, he'd nearly fallen backwards off the step, wondering if he had knocked on the wrong door due to his own weariness and the dark stormy night.

Then those beautiful green eyes had widened in surprise and it had taken all of his strength not to react. For a second, he'd seen relief in those eyes, and in that moment, he knew Terri had been right.

Jessie still cared.

But the welcomed realization hadn't made him oblivious to her gaunt appearance and the clothes that hung off her small frame like a wire hanger. Seeing that kind of dramatic weight loss had hit him like a fist in the gut, and the blunt, kneejerk observation had just popped out of his mouth.

He wished Terri would have better prepared him for the sight of his ex-wife. *Jessie isn't well,* she'd said in her voicemail. Not well? Jessie looked beyond frail. Nearly anorexic. Never mind the darkness under her eyes that looked such a blatant contrast against her naturally pale skin.

What had happened to her in the last year? His parents had seen her several weeks ago, hadn't they? Her appearance certainly couldn't have escaped Luke's ever-watchful attention. Yet they hadn't said anything in their voicemails about Jessie looking ill. And what about Brody? Matt spoke to his son at least twice a week when he wasn't restricted by a blackout. Didn't anyone think he'd care?

Apparently not.

The idea of terminal illness drifted through his mind and he gripped the counter hard, glaring at his reflection. He must have aged twenty years in those few minutes on the porch because he looked weathered and old. Middle-aged. Done in.

No wonder she'd started crying.

He set his mouth in a determined frown and walked into the adjacent bedroom they'd once shared that smelled distinctly of her subtle, sweet perfume. He glanced at the perfectly made bed. Wondered if she still slept on the left side. Happy memories from long ago tore at him as he jerked their closet open and looked for a shirt. He spotted several in the corner, along with her unused suede coat with dust buildup on the shoulders that separated her clothes from his.

Yanking a dark t-shirt off its hanger, he pulled it over his head before shifting his gaze to the details of the room, the placement of the oak furniture and the familiar bedspread of cream, navy, and gold patterns. She hadn't changed anything since he'd left, and the possibilities of what that might mean weren't lost on him. He took a deep, soul-searching breath. Maybe she hadn't moved on. Maybe she'd been waiting for him to catch up, to make a move.

But make a move in what direction? They were divorced. He had no right to ask about her health, much less, if she needed his help.

If the past had taught him anything, he didn't dare barge in and try to take over again. Terri had told him to keep his big mouth shut and listen. Not his strong suit most of the time, which was probably why she made a point to mention it.

How did one begin to make up for twelve years of starts and stops that had finally ended in the most permanent stop possible? Of course, hindsight was twenty-twenty. Quitting college and joining the Marine Corps to better support his family had probably been his biggest lapse in judgment to date. His career had ultimately cost him his marriage.

She was to join him after Basic. That had been the plan. But the tenuous foreign issues being what they were had changed the playing field, and thanks to living his entire life on a ranch with five, firearm-enthusiast brothers, his superiors quickly discovered his ability as a crack shot and pushed him toward Force Recon training. Before he knew it, time had slipped through his fingers. When he found himself listening to his infant son's cries through a static-filled phone overseas, he realized *sooner* had become *later*. Much later.

Still, he'd made a very good living in the military, and

had doubled that working for Sentry, the privately held securities firm that had recruited him the second he'd retired. Now they—rather, *Jessie*—owned the house he'd once been terrified they'd lose. To that scared, twenty-year-old, father-to-be he'd once been it felt like enough. Finally, enough.

Yeah. When he looked back, he knew that he'd made the responsible choice, but with his whole heart and to the very depths of his soul, he wished he'd made a different one. It had been that realization a month ago that had brought him to this point. His ex-wife was obviously sick, and he could only hope the fatigue of being a...well, *single* parent to a willful child with Asperger's Syndrome had caused the changes. He didn't usually consider their parenting arrangement in those terms, but he couldn't avoid the truth any longer. She was a single mom and had been at least half of their son's life. He could hardly pretend to be a fulltime father simply because he'd been available by phone.

Starting tonight, he planned to change that.

He stalked into the bathroom, grabbed his wet shirt off the counter and hung it over the shower door. He'd play the I-left-my-shirt-here routine to come around again if he had to. Staring at his haggard reflection, he blew out a breath and squared his shoulders, resolute.

Time to cowboy up.

CHAPTER TWO

She heard his slowing steps in the foyer and figured she'd save him the trouble of looking for her. "In here!" She continued pouring hot water into two mugs, steeling herself as his steps grew louder before he rounded the corner and came to an abrupt stop. Refusing to turn and look at him, she focused on the task of placing the kettle back onto the stove. When she carefully grabbed the two ceramic cups of steaming tea, he was at her side in an instant.

"Let me help."

"That's all right. It's only tea." She avoided his helping hand and stepped past him on her way to the small dining table. Carrying two mugs of hot tea gave her an excuse not to face him just yet. Best she kept her head about her if she planned to get through this evening in one, sane piece. Especially given the already difficult topic of their son.

Experience had her mentally preparing for the worst as she tried for a smile. She should give him a chance to talk. He'd once been her husband. He was Brody's father. She could at least give him a moment of her time to say whatever he'd come here to say.

She placed both cups onto the oak table and settled

herself in a chair, keeping her back to him as he brushed past her shoulder and took a seat next to her.

"This was nice of you," he said, his mouth curling up at the corner.

"And unexpected," she finished for him. He'd all but said the words.

"Well," he grinned, "the hospitality is still appreciated." For a man devoted to his coffee—just black, thanks—Matt looked awkward as he picked up the delicate teabag string and dipped the bag several times into the hot water before wrapping long fingers around the mug and testing the green brew. Swallowing, he gave her a quick smile and finally relaxed in the chair. She watched a scattering of goose bumps cover his arms and chided herself for making him stand out in the rain.

"It was the least I could do," she said, forcing levity into her voice, "since I'll probably be responsible for a massive bronchial infection tomorrow."

He tapped the tip of his finger on the cup repeatedly. If he were anyone else, she might say he looked nervous. "A sacrifice I'm happy to make," he said, dimple showing. "Your company is easily worth it."

She studied him, ever wary when those piercing blue eyes considered her a little too long. Looking away, she stared at her tea that morphed into an eerie, dark cloud.

"I like the hair, by the way," he said in an obvious attempt to keep the somewhat easy-going air between them. "Even better than curls. Brings out your eyes. Makes you look twenty."

She gave him a courtesy smile as she examined his contagious grin, drawn to his charm despite the past friction between them. "Are you trying to get on my good side?"

He let out a short laugh. "I can't be the only one to say as much."

No, but she remembered how he'd loved her curls. Then, two months ago when she'd lost too much weight too quickly, she'd discovered handfuls of hair on her pillow and the shower floor. When her remaining hair had started to break and lose its luster, a customer had mentioned chemo. That's when she'd decided to layer it and straighten the curls. It was the only way to keep anyone else from noticing. "Thanks," she said.

The following silence made seconds feel like minutes. He stayed quiet as she sensed the wheels turning in that intelligent mind of his. Twice he looked as though he might say something but he didn't. After the third time, she finally asked. "Are you waiting for me to start?"

"I thought I'd let you go first."

"Let me go first with what?"

"If you have anything you'd like to tell me," he said, "I'm here to listen."

What on earth was he talking about? Matt never listened. Much of his profession entailed organizing and giving orders. Knowing that lives depended on his ability to do that, she'd managed to hold her tongue through most of their marriage when that take-charge part of him rolled over into their personal lives.

She'd hoped they could talk about whatever he'd come here to discuss like two rational human beings, but the conversation had already turned awkward. "I don't want to be rude, Matt, but *you* came to see *me*, remember? I'm assuming you had something specific to discuss."

"Okay," he said, flipping the tea paper between his fingers with that pent-up energy again, "let's talk about your health."

"My *health?*" Her stomach churned at the idea of discussing her diagnosis. Matt would think her weak. Maybe even use that information to take Brody away from her.

"Oh, come on, Jess. Be straight with me. You look like a reed. A strong wind could blow you over. Why do you always have to act tough when obviously—"

"I'm fine," she interrupted. "And be careful with the

comments. You're lucky I let you in the door the first time with that crack."

"It was an *observation*," he said. "A kneejerk reaction when I saw you."

"Some women would kill you for that kneejerk observation."

"Stalling won't make me leave quicker, you know."

She gripped her cup with both hands. Knew that he was right. "Then we're agreed. No health questions. Let's change the subject, shall we?" She refused to look at him and took a long drink of the too-hot tea before placing the cup hard on the table. She pushed the ceramic cup forward. Pulled it back. Twisted it in circles.

"Fine," he said after watching the little ritual for nearly a minute. "Let's talk about Brody then. Can I ask how he's doing? Or is that subject off limits, too?"

She ignored his sarcasm. "What did he tell you the last time you talked?"

"Are we going to have a conversation?" he said. "Or are you planning to dodge everything I ask?" His hand dropped to the table as a line of fatigue creased his forehead. "Look, you may not agree, but I *am* trying here, Jess."

"I can see that," she said. "I guess I'm wondering why."

"Does there have to be a reason?"

Yes, and it would help if he would tell her flat out instead of doing this flanking maneuver he'd never tried in the past. He'd always been direct. Painfully blunt. This subtle nudging for information was a new move and she didn't trust it.

"Okay then," he said, gripping his mug with both hands. "How can I put this? If I'm going to be more involved in his life, I need to know where Brody is at in his studies, and *your* version of Brody's progress is usually significantly different from his. I'd like to take a bigger role with him. To do that, I need answers, and I'd prefer those answers based in reality. I'm asking you how he's doing and I need an honest reply. What are his teachers saying? That sort of thing."

Wait. *Teachers?*

"He told me he tried out for basketball," he continued. "That he made the team. He seemed pretty stoked about it, so I thought maybe—"

"The *team?*"

The all-too-familiar disappointment crossed his features and he exhaled slowly. "Let me guess. He didn't make the team?"

Among other things. *Teachers*, he'd said. The *basketball team.* All pointing to Brody attending public school, which he hadn't for weeks.

Trusting Brody in the past had never turned out well, but this time, it had been a colossal mistake. Her son had begged her to let him tell his dad about the new home schooling situation. To tell him how well he was doing. Deep down, she had hoped his new enthusiasm for studying would shine through his voice and help ease her traditional husband into accepting homeschool as a feasible option for Brody's education.

But clearly, Brody hadn't said a word, and had she known the task of telling Matt would befall her, she would have preferred doing it over the phone where she wouldn't have to witness his reaction in person. She'd had enough of his and all of Violet Valley's disapproval to last her a lifetime. "No, he didn't make the team."

He stared at a space between them, never quite meeting her gaze. "I guess I probably knew that." His mouth pulled into a thin line when he finally looked at her. "You know, I think your suggestion when we divorced that I get my information from Brody or my parents might have been a bit premature. If Brody refuses to tell me the truth and my parents rarely see you, then maybe we need to start talking again."

She couldn't imagine weekly conversations with him

but she could hardly tell him no. "That's fair."

"Tell me what happened."

"With what?"

"At tryouts. Or did he try out?"

"He did. Without telling me, of course, since I never would have allowed him to go out for a sport with his inability to handle competition. Guess the coach knows better now, too." She hated their catch-up ritual. Same conversation. Different week. Different year. "Brody wasn't ten minutes into the tryouts when another kid laughed at his technique and Brody threw the ball at him. Nearly broke the boy's nose. Blood flew everywhere and they had to take the other student to the emergency room. The coach had to remove Brody to the principal's office and the school demanded I leave work to pick him up. Again."

The ticking clock on the wall filled the usual silence that always followed her version of things. Matt had such a poker face that it was impossible to read him. He *had* to be upset. Each time she caught her son lying to her—a good portion of his waking hours—she felt the hurt and frustration all over again, like a festering wound to the heart that never healed.

"I'm sorry," she said. "I know that you've wanted him to have friends and be part of sports. To be like the other kids. To have a childhood like yours."

"It's not that," he said, hunching over the table. "I don't understand why he lies about everything. I mean, he has to know I'll find out the truth. My parents are bound to say something. Or you. We haven't talked in a year but we would eventually. I'd certainly figure it out when I visit and he's not on the team. This is impossible to hide, so why lie about it?"

"His psychologist insists that his chronic lying is part of the disorder. That Brody makes decisions based on the current moment without future consequences in mind."

Strain deepened the small lines between his eyebrows.

"In the right circumstance, that thinking could get him killed."

His comment didn't faze her; although it might have, had her ex not spent a decade of his life in the military. Matt thought through every detail of every action. His life pivoted around logic, of cause and effect. And sometime over the last decade, he'd lost his ability to see anything around him without that life-or-death lens over it.

"I'll need to talk to him about this," he said. "I had hoped we could have five minutes of good before we got into the problem issues."

"You can still do that."

"No, he lied to me." He raked a hand through his short hair and sat back. "I have to deal with it."

Not a day went by that she didn't have to contend with one of Brody's issues, one of his lies. She understood her ex-husband's disappointment. "I'm sorry, Matt. But there's more."

His wary gaze pivoted to her.

"If Brody lied to you about basketball, then he obviously left out a more important detail about school."

"He's not failing again, is he?"

"No, actually he's doing quite well. But that's only because I pulled him out of Oak Field," she said, blunt because there was no other way to say it.

"Pulled him out?" His face lost all expression. "What does that mean?"

"I…um," her mouth went dry as chalk, "removed him from public school."

"You *what?*"

The stunned betrayal in his voice made her look away, even though pulling Brody from public school had been the right thing to do.

"Why the hell would you do that?" he asked.

"Because I—"

"When?" he interrupted, not giving her a chance to respond. "How could you do that without talking to me

first?"

"It was over a month ago. After Brody asked me about the age requirement to quit school. He's been miserable since first grade, Matt. You haven't been around to see it. You don't know what it's been like for him. Or for me."

"This isn't the time to take shots at me, Jess. Just because I haven't been here every step of the way doesn't mean—"

"Yes it does," she said. "It means exactly that. And I'm not taking a shot at you. But it happens to be the truth. Look, let's stick to the subject of Brody. This is about him. About his happiness. Please remember that. Try to keep an open mind."

"I *have* an open mind," he said. "But you didn't give me a chance, did you? You lied."

"I didn't lie. I simply didn't tell you because Brody wanted to be the one to break the news. He begged me. And then he told me you were happy with his progress. That you were okay with the new arrangement. How was I to know he didn't say anything?"

"Let me think," he said. "Maybe because he has a history of chronic lying? Look, you *know* me, Jess. It never occurred to you I'd have a problem with this?"

Deep down she'd known, and guilt stabbed at her as she turned from his accusing eyes. "Well maybe. I don't know. You're gone so often it's easy to forget how difficult you can be." Grabbing her half-empty mug, she stood and headed back to the kitchen, hands shaking.

His chair squeaked when he rose to follow her.

"This type of news should never have been entrusted to Brody to tell me," he said. "What's worse, you removed him from school without asking me. You can't make important decisions like this about *our* son without talking to me. At least give me that much consideration."

The lump in her throat tightened. Self-preservation had her wanting to leave, but she was determined to get through this. She grabbed the kettle and started pouring hot water into her cup, stopping abruptly when it overflowed onto her fingers. "Ouch!"

He made a move toward her but she lifted her palm, stopping him from crossing the kitchen. "It's fine," she said, rubbing her wet, sore fingers against her jeans. "I'm fine."

He braced his hand against the corner wall. "So who's teaching him then?"

"I am."

He probably couldn't have looked more stunned if she'd thrown an iron skillet at his head. "You never finished your degree. You need certification to be a teacher."

"I don't need certification to homeschool my own son," she told him, voice shaking despite her effort to sound in command.

"To homeschool *my* son you do."

"*Our* son," she corrected. "And no. I don't. I finished two years of college. I'm not *dumb*, Matt."

"I never said you were."

"Then put that pride of yours aside for once and trust me on this. I'm doing everything correctly. Documenting his grades through a nearby academy. He'll take the state tests every year. The academy even provides scheduled outdoor activities to promote social skills, although I haven't enrolled him in any of those because he's too busy at the ranch. Besides, his social abilities—"

"Will never improve as long as you keep doing this overprotective mom thing by hiding him from other students his age."

"I'm not hiding him. I'm giving him a breath. And it's working, Matt. His grades have already improved. More importantly, he's happy. He's even enjoying learning Spanish."

He blinked, looking dumbstruck. "I wasn't aware you spoke Spanish."

She squared her shoulders. "Well, I do."

"Since when?"

"I'm…learning."

He leaned one broad shoulder against the doorframe and folded his arms over his chest. "So, that would be a no."

"Spanish is *one* thing I'm teaching him, and it's an elective. And in only a few weeks, we've gained more ground in math and writing than he has in over year. He'd slipped two full grades in both subjects, and the teachers couldn't get past his behavior problems to teach him. So I got rid of the middleman and I'm doing it myself. He had excellent teachers, but they just couldn't control his environment with hundreds of other kids. But I can control it here. I can make sure he learns what he needs to know."

"Jess—"

"Don't you dare fight me on this, Matt. They've practically crippled him with that autistic label. It's his get-out-of-everything card, and I couldn't take it anymore. He's smart. He can learn. He can be anything he wants to be, but he needs more time and attention than they can give him."

"And you can give him that kind of attention while working twelve-hour days?"

"My point exactly," she said. "I work ten to twelve hours each day and I *still* spend more time with him than his teachers ever could. What does that tell you?"

"It tells me you're working too hard and not thinking straight. That's what it tells me. Most parents bring up these types of issues with the School Board. But you? You pull him from school. Why didn't you just talk to the Board?"

"Oh right," she said. "That's what I want to do. Take on the School Board, as if I don't already have enough going on. I have a shop to run and enough weekly meetings regarding our son that I can't get to them all. I've been doing this since he was two, Matt. That's ten years of doctors and psychologists. Of quarterly IEP meetings and weekly behavior monitoring sessions. Of putting our child on so many pills to suppress his disorder that I can't possibly have a clue of what Brody's true personality is anymore. Drugs I'm required to give him to keep him in Special Services, and the entire time they can't make the smallest of headway with him." She braced a hand on her hip. "Well, enough is enough. Brody is off the medication, and for once in ten years, I'm gaining ground with our son."

"You sound like it's been decided. Like we're done talking about this."

She huffed out a sigh. "That's because we are."

A humorless grin pulled at the corners of his mouth. "Oh, believe me. We're not done talking. Not by a long shot."

Recognizing the fix-it look on his face, she crossed her arms over her chest. "I will *not* let you do this again."

"Do what again?"

"Come in and disrupt everything. You have no idea what this has been like for me. You're gone and I'm here, and long after you leave again, I'll be dealing with all of this—"

"I told you I'm back for good," he interrupted, pulling away from the doorframe. "I'll *be* here this time to help. What do I have to say to make you believe that?"

"Possibly," she said, as years of resentment bubbled to the surface. "Or *probably*. They're words without meaning to me. Seriously, what are you going to do with your life, if not what you're currently doing? Admit it. You love it, Matt. A fact made ever so apparent by your increasing difficulty when you're here."

He shook his head once. "Meaning?"

"Meaning you gauge everything like there's some life-or-death consequence. Go here. Step there. As though there's a sniper in the church balcony or a bomb in the hardware store planter. Every time you come home, you're more withdrawn. More cautious. You struggle repeatedly to integrate back into a town and society you've sworn to protect. You pretend you're happy here, Matt, but the truth is you can't wait to leave again."

"That's not true and you know it. I've always hated leaving my family behind—"

"I don't know any such thing," she interrupted with a shake of her head. "And I can't help thinking that all of this would be so much easier if you'd just admit it to yourself once and for all."

"Admit *what?*"

"That regular life is no longer comfortable for you. You're secretive, Matt. And paranoid. For petesake, you even worry someone in town will take a picture of you and post it on social media. You won't attend a single social gathering—"

"There's a reason I can't have people taking pictures of me, Jess."

"I know. It's for your safety. I get it."

"Never mind *my* safety. I worry about yours and Brody's safety. My family's safety. My team's safety. There are people out there who can't see my face and know my real name or where I live."

"You do realize there are people who don't live like this," she said with another sigh, rubbing the creases from her forehead. "You know that, right?" Her gaze met his again. "Should I mention the nightmares you pretend you don't have? The nights you wake in a cold sweat? The early morning hours you pace the house as though you're on some kind of dawn patrol?" His eyes widened. "Did you think I didn't know? That I couldn't see? Matt, most people would need a therapist if they'd seen what you've seen. But not you. *You* take a couple of aspirin and run back to it as fast as you can." Pain churned in her stomach, reminding her that she needed to calm down before her blood pressure skyrocketed again. "One phone call from Max—an assignment no one else will do—and you're out the door. So guess what? I don't believe you're here to stay. I don't. And after the years I've spent watching you walk out that door, you have no right to act surprised that I'm certain you'll do it again."

It was more than she'd ever said on the matter, much less *yelled*, and the raw pain that flashed in his eyes briefly left her doubting herself.

"Wow," was all he said.

One word said in that gentle, contemplative tone and she felt monumentally ashamed of herself. "I shouldn't have said that," she whispered quickly, looking away as she forced herself to get some perspective. She should be thanking God he was here at all. He hadn't died. He wasn't sick. He was home. Safe. It was all she'd wanted for thirteen years. Why couldn't she just be happy about it? Just take his promise for face value and enjoy two seconds of relief without assuming doom and gloom would naturally follow. Try as she might, she couldn't do that. Perhaps this would be her reality forever. Perhaps she would never be free of the panic that gutted her every time she thought of him out there.

"I'm sorry," he said. "I had no idea you felt that way."

She slid a guilty glance at him. "Well, it's not *all* I feel, Matt. I respect what you do. Surely, you know that. Your devotion to your country. It's inspiring and I admire you for it, despite the fact that you chose it over me."

"I didn't choose it over you."

"Oh right." She pressed fingers against the pain exploding in her stomach. "I'd love to pretend we're going to resolve *that* argument again."

"Why can't you just believe me?"

"Put yourself in my shoes, Matt, and answer that question."

His Adam's apple bobbed as he stared at her. "Okay. Granted, some of what you said is true. I promised you a different life. This wasn't it. And I can't say anything to that except I'm sorry. But that's behind us. I'm retiring this time. For good. And going forward I'll be here. A fulltime parent. You don't have to do all of it by yourself anymore."

She turned from his gaze, holding herself as conflicting emotions clogged her throat. She wanted this. To believe him. So badly.

"If we keep talking," he said, "we can get past this wall we keep hitting. It *is* possible, Jess, that we could both be part of Brody's life without trying to kill each other." He came away from the refrigerator and walked around the island, moving into her space. "Just work with me. It's all I'm asking."

She looked at him. "Work with you? With what?"

"Let's try putting Brody back in school. With both of us helping him, he can catch up on the time he missed. It's not too late. Give me a chance to fix this."

"This," she repeated, ever the idiot until it dawned on her what he meant. "Fix my mistake of pulling him out you mean?"

His eyebrows came together. "That's not what I meant."

"Really?" she asked. "Then what did you mean?"

"I'm saying Brody's education is important to me."

She took a step away from him, the small of her back pressing the edge of the counter. "And it isn't to me? Do you think this is the easier route for me to take? That I *like* working twelve-hour days while playing the role of mother, teacher, and *father* to my son?"

"I know it's been hard for you. That's why I want to help."

"Except that your idea of helping is by dismantling everything I've done. Thanks but no thanks." Pushing away from the counter, she walked past him and out of the kitchen.

He followed her. "Would you quit doing that walking-away thing you always do?"

"Sure," she shot over her shoulder, "when you quit

doing that taking-over thing *you* always do." She maneuvered quickly around the sofa, desperate to put space between them.

"Stop walking away from me, Jess!"

She'd made it halfway to the hallway when she halted stock-still, stunned by the raw edge of emotion in a command that practically vibrated the air. Her lingering irritation had a small part of her wanting to pivot in mock salute, to remind him she didn't work as an operative in one of his units. But she couldn't do that. Not after hearing the desperate thread of panic in his voice.

"Please." His voice sounded low, uncertain. "Don't leave like this. I don't want to yell anymore. Or argue with you. Stay. Please. Just talk to me."

She gripped her elbows again, hugging herself at the exhausting notion of going another round with him. Her emotions were scattered. Stretched too thin. She turned, tears in her eyes as she spotted him at the edge of the living room, his usual frown in place. "I *did* talk to you, Matt. To no avail. I've told you more than I've ever dared and you've wasted no time in running over me as though I'm an observer in this whole thing. Don't you realize how often you do this? Every time you come home, you walk in and erase everything I've accomplished."

"What does that even mean?"

"What in all of that was confusing?"

"I've told you more than I've ever dared," he said, repeating her words back to her slowly. "What is that supposed to mean?"

Unable to believe she'd said the words out loud, she could only stare at him until the sound of a key in the door interrupted, followed by a boy's giggle, and a man's muffled voice.

He turned to the door.

"That would be Brody," she said.

"Not just Brody." He turned to her with an arched brow. "Who's with him?"

"Cole." She swallowed hard.

"Cole?" Confusion quickly dissipated. "Cole McLeod?"

She nodded. "That's where Brody's been tonight. He wanted to view a jail cell up close. Cole said he'd take him."

Poor Matt had no time to consider what that meant as Brody—babbling and sounding certain he recognized his dad's SUV in the dark—entered the house and abruptly stopped talking when he spotted his father in the flesh. "Dad!" Brody grinned broadly, as Cole stepped into the foyer behind him to see the impromptu reunion, hat in hand and blonde hair disheveled as though he'd run his hand through it.

Brody's excitement faded when he turned to his mom standing by the sofa, arms crossed over her chest and probably looking a little red-eyed as she tried for a smile.

"Hey, sweetie," she said. "How was the trip?"

"Have you been crying, Mom?" Brody's expression tightened as he looked back to his dad. "What'd you say to her?"

CHAPTER THREE

"Brody—" Matt stopped the reprimand; he didn't want the first thing out of his mouth to be something negative. He hadn't seen his son for two months and he especially didn't want to make a show of family dysfunction in front of Cole McLeod. Bad enough the child's elation at seeing him had morphed into a suspicious scowl.

Matt's gaze shifted to Cole—one of his oldest friends—standing in full police uniform by the door. When he caught the cryptic glance between Cole and Jessie, he wondered if he'd imagined the exchange. But Jessie looked uncomfortable and nervous as she turned and began to pace by the sofa. Jealousy did a slow burn through his veins. Coupled with the unsavory feeling of looking like a third wheel in his own home, he struggled against an overwhelming desire to show his old friend through the front door.

"Sorry," Brody mumbled, turning Matt's attention back to his son, who had the good sense to look apologetic now for overstepping with his earlier question. The boy must have grown at least an inch or more since he'd last seen him. Lanky, skinny, with a dark fringe of hair he flicked over his eyebrows as he looked up at Matt with familiar blue eyes. "Mom was just talking about you the other day. She said—"

"*Brody,*" Jessie said, clearing her throat loudly and pulling their son's attention to where she still stood in the living area. She looked tense and uneasy, but the boy only stared at her, questioning her expression and body language that would be obvious to anyone without Asperger's Syndrome.

Brody turned to Matt as if asking him to translate—a typical response for his son, who usually talked incessantly and often said too much without realizing it. "What's the big secret?" the boy said with a shrug. "She just said you'd do everything you could to get here by Christmas. How long can you stay?"

Matt turned to Jessie for some hint of how much to tell his son, but he caught an apologetic glance from her to Cole instead. Matt turned to the other man, curious how long the recent widower had been spending time with Matt's family and helping himself to his front door.

"Permanently," Matt said, staring at Cole McLeod when he said it. "I'm home permanently."

"R-really?" A tremor in Brody's voice turned Matt's attention back to his son, whose mouth quivered while he watched his dad with wide eyes, as though he were looking at a ghost. He could never have anticipated the news would cause such a serious, stricken expression. He knew the kid was sensitive, that he felt things deeply, but nothing could have prepared him for those watering eyes and trembling chin. Suddenly, as if he couldn't stop himself, Brody took a step forward and threw his skinny arms around him in a powerful hug that nearly squeezed the air out of his lungs. Matt's breath caught in his throat, more out of surprise than the crush-hold his son had on him. "You're staying for good?" Brody murmured with a near-sob against his shirt, hiding his face. "Seriously?"

Folding his arms around his son, he ran a hand through the kid's mop of hair, the boy's dramatic response causing regret to grip him by the throat. Yet another reminder that his absences had affected his family more deeply than he'd realized. "Yeah, kiddo. I'm here for good." Had it only been the two of them without Cole and Jessie looking on, he might have let go of a tear or two himself. Instead, he kissed the top of Brody's head, pulling himself together as he looked to Jessie. The color had drained from her face and she chewed her thumbnail now as she studied their son's reaction.

Brody pulled back from the hug to look up at his dad. "You promise? You're moving back? You and mom are back together?"

Whoa—what?

"Your dad is staying at the ranch, honey," Jessie interjected, immediately nixing the idea before the boy's imagination created a family utopia where one didn't exist.

"Your grandparents need me at the ranch for a big project," Matt added. "But I'll see you every day. I promise."

Jessie grunted a sound of disapproval, but Brody's grin was all that mattered. "Could we go to another game?" the child blurted. "Or maybe we can go to the new wall climbing thing at the mall. I've wanted to try it, but Mom won't take me. Maybe we could—"

Matt laughed as he hugged Brody tighter. The child never stopped talking after that, babbling about all the things they could do, and from the sound of it, preferably all of them tomorrow. But the joy of finally feeling welcome didn't last as Jessie turned and began to pace again.

What had she expected? For him to hand over his house key to Cole McLeod?

When hell froze over.

"Listen, Brody," Matt said, pulling from the hug to look down at his son. "It's late. Why don't you thank Cole—Officer McLeod—for his time tonight, and we can talk about everything in the morning." He nodded to Cole, who smiled only when Brody turned to him.

"Always my pleasure, sport," McLeod said with a curt nod. "You'll make a great addition to the program." Brody's proud grin at the man's use of the endearment spoke volumes about the relationship there. Matt's eyes had narrowed by the time McLeod looked at him. "Good to see you home safe, Matt."

"Thanks." The poacher somehow managed to sound sincere, which probably had more to do with Jessie than any true happiness he felt about Matt's return home. How often did this interloper spend time with his son, anyway? And what program were they talking about?

Brody offered his hand to McLeod like a man. Cole took it in a firm grip and nodded again while murmuring something about seeing himself out.

"Thanks again, Cole," Jessie said, quickly catching up to him at the door. "Drive safe." An awkward delay between the two told Matt he hadn't been wrong. *Something* was going on, and it killed him to stand there and watch it. When Cole leaned in as if to kiss her cheek, Jessie quickly shoved her hand out to him. The other man glanced at Matt briefly, accepted the handshake, holding her hand a little too long before turning on his heel and out the door.

She closed the front door and leaned against it.

The rain had stopped sometime during the last hour, but another storm was brewing inside. "Cole McLeod?" he said. "Are you kidding me, Jess? He's one of my oldest friends."

"Well, he's one of my oldest friends, too," she said, her gaze not reaching his. "So? He spends time with Brody."

"Jess—"

"I'm not about to discuss this with you."

Brody looked to his mom, then back to his dad. "Are you guys about to argue?"

"No," they both said in unison over his head.

"Because it sounds like you are."

They stared at each other briefly before Jessie looked to

Brody. "We're not fighting, sweetie. And we're not *going* to fight either. Your dad is leaving and you need to get ready for bed."

"We're not done talking," Matt said.

She looked up at him, that pretty face morphing into a tired frown. "We can finish another time."

"Let's finish tonight," he said, not really asking. She at least owed him an explanation as to why Cole McLeod had taken Brody to observe a jail cell up close. How could he be the only one who took issue with this?

"It's late," she said.

"It's not even my bedtime," Brody pointed out.

"Look, I realize we're not fixing this overnight," Matt agreed, "but we have things to discuss."

"Fixing this?" she said. "I told you there's nothing to fix."

"Mom?"

"It's a word, Jess. Quit taking it personally."

"Mom?"

Distracted, she looked to their son. "Brody, why aren't you going to bed?"

"You're sure you're okay, Mom?" he asked, real concern in his voice.

"I'm fine." She looked at Matt, bugging her eyes at him as if to say *see what you've done* before pacing to the window. The kid rarely interpreted a social cue correctly, especially with sarcasms and half-truths flying through the air, so the boy stayed glued to the spot, staring at her back while waiting for a better answer that wouldn't contradict her tone.

"Go on," Matt said. "Your mom is okay, I promise. Get moving. I'll see you in the morning."

Brody paused. "Will you stay tonight?"

Matt shook his head and nodded in the direction of the kid's bedroom. "But I'll be by in the morning to take you to breakfast."

"He has school," Jessie said, turning from the window.

"He also needs to eat."

"Woot! Awesome! Breakfast!" Brody took two steps to go but turned and ran back to him for another quick hug. "I'm glad you're home, Dad," he said, then gave him a goofy grin and shot off to the other end of the house. "Goodnight!"

"Straight to bed after brushing your teeth!" Jessie called after him. "I'd better not catch you sneaking out to watch TV or eavesdrop on our conversation."

"Okay!" he yelled, an excited lilt in his voice.

The flurry of noise and action left as the whirlwind child made his exit complete. Matt turned to Jessie as soon as Brody's bedroom door closed. "So. *McLeod*. What's that about?"

She looked weary and tired of looking at him. "What about him?"

"I'm not stupid, Jessica. How long? Before or after the divorce?"

The use of her full name was never a good idea. Adding serious insult to injury by questioning her fidelity while they were married was a desperate dig, but he couldn't help it. Jealousy burned in his veins like acid. He needed the truth and making her mad was usually a good way to get it.

Her hands went to her hips as she squared off with him. "Okay, first, is there something wrong with his name?"

"No."

"Then quit saying it like that."

"Like what?"

"Like you're talking about smallpox or SARS."

He shrugged.

"And if you want me to keep talking to you, don't use my full name. You know I hate it." She held up a finger, pointing it at him. "And *don't* go letting that big brain of yours make all of this more complicated than it is. I have enough problems in my life. I won't let you make Brody's relationship with Cole one of them."

"Brody's relationship with Cole isn't what I'm concerned about. It's yours."

"We're friends."

He forced out a blunt laugh. "I've seen you as friends. That wasn't friendship. Thaaat was something else."

"You are really making me mad, you know that?"

"Tough."

"Maybe you don't get how divorce works, Matt. A divorce means that you don't have any say in my personal life anymore."

Ah. Now *that* sounded like Jessie—drawing lines in the sand and telling him where to go if he didn't comply. Combined with that finger she pointed at him—something she knew he disliked with a passion—it felt like coming home. "Has he proposed?"

"What?"

"You heard me."

"Are you insane? We've been on a few dates."

The knife twisted deeper. "What's a few?"

"I'm not having this conversation with you," she said. "Look, Brody already thinks we're fighting—"

"We're not fighting," he said. "We're finally talking."

"Sounds like arguing to me. You always did confuse the two."

"No confusion. We do everything passionately, Jess. It's what we do."

Her gaze dropped briefly to his chest and her cheeks turned pink. She turned, gripped the front door handle and swung the thing wide, motioning him out with a hand. "I have work tomorrow."

"Fine. I'll be by in the morning to take Brody out to breakfast."

"Hey, Hard-of-Hearing," she said as she grabbed his Stetson off the small table and shoved it at him. "I said it's a school day tomorrow."

"So?" He pulled the hat slightly down his forehead and

grinned at her, supremely smug to be making a dent in that tough exterior. "Isn't that one of the reasons you decided to homeschool him? So you could have more flexibility?" He walked around her and through the door, sensing her annoyed glare following him down step for step. Once his boots touched gravel, he turned to see her silhouette in the doorway, haloed by the light from the foyer. She perched her hands on her hips, and when his eyes adjusted to the different light, he noticed her sweet mouth twisted in a frown. Something about that stance brought out the devil in him, and he couldn't help but challenge her once more. "Right?"

"Let me tell you something, Matthew Aaron Brewer," she said, revealing a hint of that southern drawl that only came out when she planned to give someone a good dressing down. He readied himself for it as she crossed the porch to point that finger at him again. "Don't you dare try to turn this homeschool situation around to your advantage, do you hear me? I will *not* let you use that against me. It is everything I can do to keep his schedule as it is—"

He took two of the three steps back up, his height just slightly over hers now, which seemed to embolden her since she didn't back up but took a step closer, needing better proximity to shove that finger at his chest. Focusing on her words was difficult as he caught the slightest tease of her perfume. He bit down to restrain a smile as she jabbed him again. Full of fire and vinegar, she looked breathtaking as she succinctly told him what she thought of him and his inability to respect her as Brody's legitimate teacher. His forced serious expression wavered when she hit full stride, calling him a few choice words and adding another quick, hard poke to his chest before she continued. "Besides, I didn't pull him out of school for you to show up here—" another poke to the chest, "—*unannounced,* I might add, so that you can pretend to have an open mind while purposefully messing up everything

I've—"

If someone would have asked him later, he probably couldn't have said what lunacy had gone through his mind during her diatribe. One minute she'd been reading him his rights like a firebrand who didn't know when to quit. A second later, he'd grabbed that finger she'd been pointing at him all night, pulled her to him, and kissed her.

She stiffened.

Pushed against him.

Grabbed his shirt.

And melted.

This was his Jessie. He loved her like this—breathing fire and giving him hell. A woman addicted to control, like him. A woman who, in the right circumstances, loved nothing more than to lose that control. To him. Her lips softened against his and he threaded his fingers through that silky hair. He had already kissed her six ways from Sunday over the years, and he intended to add a *then-some* to that when he deepened the kiss with a longing he could never, on his most articulate day, put into words. And then she was kissing him back, her hands clutching his shirt as her tongue danced against his with a yearning that matched his own. His hands gripped her waist, and for the briefest, craziest moment, he thought maybe…

She pulled her mouth away with a sharp intake of breath. "Matt—"

He opened his eyes, his mind still on the fringe of reality, trying to remember they were divorced. That she was no longer his wife. He expected her to take a step back but she didn't. Instead, her mouth lingered close to his, as if she wasn't sure about this divorce debacle any more than he was. He watched her gaze drop to his lips again, her breaths still coming hard, mingling with his as she whispered his name a second time, and before he could talk himself out of it, he lowered his mouth once more to hers. He kissed her softly, only a moment, before she pulled away with a slight push to his chest, her flushed cheeks making those eyes flash a beautiful passion-filled green as she whispered, "This is wrong, Matt."

Nothing about how she felt in his arms could be wrong. But she was right. This wasn't the time or place; they had a million things to work out. "I should probably go," he said softly.

She nodded, looked down and took a step back.

Fighting his need to hold her again, he turned to give her the space she wanted, barely making it down the stairs when she said, "I'm sorry."

He stopped and turned to her, noticing that her flannel shirt had dropped to her elbows during that kiss as she awkwardly pulled the material back over her shoulders. His mouth went dry as he got a good glimpse of her. Without the flannel, her tank top revealed the stark signs of poor health. Her arms, once tone with muscle, were skinny and fragile. Goose bumps covered his skin as the cool night air drifted past them, and when she visibly shivered, he recalled the outline of her ribs when his hand had glided over her side.

A knot of protectiveness tightened in his gut. "Me too," he said abruptly, probably because he wasn't sorry. "I didn't exactly plan that."

"I know." She pulled at the material again as though somehow trying to cover herself twice. "It was…habit."

He yanked off his hat and kneaded the brim, unsure how to respond to that. "If you say so." He couldn't say a single thing that didn't sound curt or irritated, probably because worrying about her health was beginning to take a serious toll on him. If he looked back far enough, he'd been worrying about her his whole life, since they were kids, when girls hadn't been a blip on his radar. She'd had a boatload dumped on her plate at an early age. By the time they'd met at thirteen, she had already traded most of her childhood to play housemaid and nurse to her drunk father, and mother to her little sister. Jessie had been a bossy thing even then. Antagonistic. *Big* chip on her shoulder. And there had been a depth and fire in those green eyes that had sucked him right in.

Now if only he could push her out of his mind and life as easily as she'd pushed him from hers.

"You okay?" she asked.

He pulled out of the thought. "Perfect." Abrupt again. "I'm perfect."

"It's just that I've never seen that expression before."

She must never have seen what totally screwed looked like on a man's face, because that summed up this new and empty life without her. Totally screwed. And there was nothing he could do about it. Not at the moment anyway. He thwacked his hat hard against his thigh, walking backward and away from the house. "Forget it. I'm tired. I'll be by at seven to pick up Brody. Goodni—

Regret and frustration choked off the word before he could finish, and he turned abruptly, pulling the Stetson onto his head as he stalked to his SUV. The interior felt cool and damp when he got behind the wheel, and he looked up to stare at the closed front door of their house and the now empty porch.

The curtain pulled back and those rounding green eyes glanced outside.

He flipped the ignition and sat staring at the house long after she disappeared behind the curtain to turn off the lights. Yeah. Totally screwed. He still cared deeply for a woman who clearly no longer wanted contact with him. To complicate the issue, there remained the matter of his job. The one he hadn't fully left yet.

Legally, he wasn't certain he could.

CHAPTER FOUR

Matt pressed his palms to the sides of the sink, looking out the kitchen window to his family's acreage shrouded in darkness. He wished sunrise would hurry. He needed a serious dose of the countryside to elevate his mood. In all his travels, he'd never found another piece of land where he'd seen this kind of beauty. Of course, sentiment might be influencing him, but at the very least, he could say the ranch had been one of the only places he'd ever found any amount of peace.

Present company notwithstanding.

His scowl actually started to hurt and he forced in a deep breath, hoping to lose the foul mood before he stopped at the house to pick up his son. Before he saw Jessie again.

He hadn't poured his first cup of coffee that morning before his mother had launched into him about Jessie and Brody, which—combined with little sleep—had immediately hit him wrong.

The imperious woman heaved a sigh of disappointment behind him. He rolled his eyes and focused on dawn just beyond the ridge. In his mind's eye, he could picture the ranch hands stumbling out of their cabins, yawning and stretching on their way to the stables and barn. He could imagine his younger sister, Tessa, standing by the pond currently dark in the distance, feeding the multitude of ducks after the morning meal while her infectious laughter traveled back to the house.

Yeah, he could count on good times here, even when the rest of his life fell apart.

"All I'm saying," Fiona Brewer said in that domineering tone, "is that this homeschooling thing is a little strange. It's not normal. That's all I'm saying. I mean, children need to play, don't they? They need to be around other children. Am I right? What am I supposed to tell my friends from church when they ask about my Brody? Why, the other day I was in the store and—"

"I said the subject isn't up for discussion," Matt interrupted, annoyed that she'd promised to let it go and hadn't. "I support Jessie in her decision to homeschool our son and that's the end of it." He didn't consider it his parents' business, or more specifically, his mother's business, whether or not he supported Jessie in anything. Fiona Brewer was an emotional, dramatic woman with an incredible knack of making everything more difficult than it had to be. His mother's input was the *last* thing he needed now, especially while trying to smooth things over with Jessie.

When he heard her tsk of disapproval, he turned and leaned against the counter, facing *the look*. From her small chair at the kitchen table, she managed to make him feel ten-years-old again by eyeing him with that critical head-to-toe glare. She'd pulled her thick, yellow hair behind her head in a tight bun this morning. Dressed in dark blue jeans and a bright blue and white western shirt, she kept one leg crossed over the other as her foot bounced in a tight rhythm, waiting in silence for him to apologize.

His dad, Stern Brewer, sat next to her, a newspaper in front of his face as he cleared his throat when the silence lasted too long.

"Matthew," she said, "you know I love Jessie—"

"We all love, Jessie," said his brother, Luke, who appeared in the kitchen doorway. He acknowledged Matt with a quick nod before looking at their mother. "Any time you begin a sentence with *you know I love so-and-so*, things usually don't end well. Probably best you don't finish that statement, Mom. Assuming you don't want to run Matt off to another war just so he can escape the criticism around here."

"I am not *Mom,*" Fiona Brewer said with a wave of her hand and roll of her eyes. "I am your mother and you will address me accordingly."

"Yes, ma'am," Luke said with a grin.

Matt was thankful for his younger brother's intrusion, whose constant needling of their mother kept the woman on her toes the entire time they were together. Leaning his weight on his cane, Luke took a step forward in time to avoid their sister, Tessa, who came barreling into the room behind him carrying a box of canned goods.

"I'm a busy girl, people. Out of my way," she said. Her long, auburn braid bounced as she made her way past the table, shooting a glance at Matt as if finally noticing him. "Glad you're back in one piece, big brother. Staying for Christmas?"

He knew better than to stand gawking at her energy, and quickly moved out of her way. She brushed past him, a flurry of movement in her usual rush to the adjacent kitchen connected by a simple swinging door.

"Don't change the subject, Tessa," Fiona sputtered.

"Glad to hear it," Tessa said with a nod, disappearing into the restaurant-sized kitchen she helped design, aptly named—*Tessa's Kitchen*. His sister had to prepare a scrumptious meal for more than twenty people this morning, and all he could do was envy her for having a place to hide from their mother's prying.

"Take off your hat, young man," their mother said, shooting her evil eye toward Luke again.

Luke's eyes crossed as he looked up to the brim of his beige hat. Doing a quick hobble to the table, he grabbed the hat and flipped it twice before hanging it on the back of a chair. Easing into a sitting position, he extended his bad leg, ran a hand through his dark blonde hair and grinned broadly at their mother. Matt had rarely seen his brother unhappy, whose constant, contagious smile and laugh transformed his features, breaking apart the scar across his left cheek and making it disappear.

"All I'm saying," Fiona said again, grabbing the silver pot on the table and pouring a cup of coffee for Luke, "is that my grandson is perfectly fine. Nothing wrong with him at all. He's my only grandson. I would know if Brody had something wrong with him, wouldn't I?"

Luke turned to Matt, looking cautiously optimistic as he waited for his response.

"The word *wrong* is an inappropriate term here, Mother," Matt said, gathering his patience as she passed the cup to his dad, who in turn slid it gingerly across the table to Luke without breaking from his paper. "Brody's disorder causes difficulties in a variety of settings, not just school. I'm home only a few months out of the year, he is my *only* child, and even I've seen some of the differences between him and other children his age. I realize you see what you prefer to see, but I'm not going to let you make an already difficult situation worse by staying in denial. This is hard enough on Jessie without her having to fight you, too. In fact, I have a good idea why she's not coming around to visit if this is the kind of grief she gets."

She looked surprised by that. "Whose side are you on?"

"My family's side," he said.

Her eyes narrowed at his use of the general term.

"Speaking of visits, when did we see Jessie last?" Luke asked, looking to their father. "In October?"

"We did not," Fiona said. "I would remember."

"That's right," Luke said. "It was November. Remember, Pop? That's when the scout troops were here."

"What?" Fiona looked aghast, turning to her husband who simply flipped another page. "Where was I?"

Luke had the devil's glint in his eyes as he leaned passed the newspaper, his expression deadpan. "As you might have guessed, she avoids you, Mother. In fact, we've been sneaking around behind your back for months."

She pursed her lips and turned from him dramatically, waving a hand to shoo him. Matt assumed that she secretly enjoyed these little battles of wills with her youngest son. Her relationship with Luke had been unique from the first, and aside from their father, Luke had been the only one able to get through that tough, barely likeable exterior of hers. He also remained one of the only people who could make her laugh.

"My children hate me," she announced stiffly, drinking her coffee. "I can't believe I'm saying this, but my children hate me."

"Oh, don't be dramatic, Mother," Luke said. "I'm joking. Jessie only stopped by for a few questions. Can I help it if I charmed her into letting Brody go riding with me while they were here?"

"Questions?" Matt repeated, arching an eyebrow.

Luke looked up. "Yeah. She borrowed a couple of my programming books. She's been designing a database…an inventory system for the shop. When she ran into a slightly advanced coding issue, it was easier to show her on the laptop than try to explain it over the phone. I convinced her to time the visit so I could take Brody riding with some of the scouts. He does much better with younger children than kids his own age. We thought it might help with his social skills."

"Brody went trail riding?" Fiona asked. "Do you mean to tell me Jessie stayed here for two to four hours and never stopped by the house to say hello to me? Why, I can't believe that. It's…well, it's rude." She turned to her husband who pulled the paper closer to his face. "I ask you, what did I do to warrant such animosity? Can someone please tell me?"

No one dared to answer that.

"Actually," Luke said, taking a swallow of coffee. "Jessie joined us. I believe you were shopping."

She eyed him suspiciously, murmuring, "How convenient."

Luke grinned. "Exactly as we planned it."

"Oh hush if you can't be serious," she said, stiffening into a rigid posture.

"You do shop often," he mentioned.

She glanced over her reading glasses at her youngest son. "I have had quite enough from you this morning, Lucas Jacob." She turned to Matt, serious. "Matthew, when do you intend to do something about this? That wife of yours needs to be a proper mother and bring my only grandson by on the weekends when I can see him."

"*Ex*-wife," Matt reminded her, unable to let the comment slide. "And she's an excellent mother. Ease up."

She grunted, finally done with her interrogation as she slid her unfinished coffee away from her and stood, grabbing her gardening hat off the counter with a quick swipe of her perfectly manicured hand. "I'm certain I have more important things to do this morning than to sit here and take this abuse from my own children."

"What abuse?" Luke asked innocently when she stepped over his extended leg on her way out, his gaze following her into the hallway. "*Mmmmoooom,*" he said, drawing out the shorter endearment she hated. "Don't be mad. You know we love you."

The mudroom door slammed.

Luke turned a wide-eyed face to Matt as though they were young again and in serious trouble. Matt couldn't help but share his smile.

"I don't know why she's so focused on socializing him with other children," Luke said. "Whenever they're together, Mother won't let him out of her sight. She likes to spoil him." He took another swallow of coffee. "Oh, speaking of stopping by, why don't you bring him 'round today, around one o'clock. Jessie, too, if you can manage it. I could use Brody's help in the arena and I'd like her to see why. Firsthand."

"And if Jessie doesn't have other plans," Stern added matter-of-fact behind his paper, "perhaps she and Brody could stay for dinner. Might make your mother happy. Just something to think about."

Luke smiled at Stern, a genuine love for their dad softening his eyes. Unlike Matt, Luke had been the perfect son. A good kid. Brilliant, too. He'd graduated high school at sixteen. By age twenty, he'd earned two degrees and entered the information technology field. A geek at heart, he'd surprised everyone when after only two years in the field, he realized his heart belonged to the ranch and returned to work for their parents. After the accident four years ago that took the regular use of his left leg and nearly took his life, he'd almost gone back to the profession. But like all Brewers, he stuck it out, retrained himself to do things differently, and managed most of his duties on the ranch very well. He only did everything at a slower pace these days, which suited his easy-going personality anyway.

"How's the, um, *programming* going?" Matt asked, hoping no one could tell by his blank expression that he had no clue what Jess did anymore with her free time, other than spending it with that ex-wife-trolling, Cole McLeod.

"She missed her calling," Luke said. "I mean, she does a great job with the shop. She's an amazing cook. But she could do anything else if she wanted to. She burned through most of the technical books I gave her as if they were shorts in fiction. Even I didn't read those things chapter by chapter the way she did. But between the shop and working with the kid to keep up his grades, I doubt she could find the time to go back to school. In fact, I think she might be hitting burnout. Looked a little skinny the last time I saw her."

"Skinny?" Matt snorted, sounding bitter. "What a kind euphemism."

"What?" Luke asked, losing his smile. "She's not sick, is she?"

Stern Brewer lowered his paper, staring at Matt over his reading glasses.

Matt shook his head. "I'm hoping it's only the strain of trying to do too much. She hasn't given me a clear answer. We're still getting...reacquainted."

Luke's eyebrows lifted. "Arguing, you mean."

"Among other things."

"Hm." A devious smile curled his brother's mouth. "Think you might work things out and get back together?"

Matt sighed and looked to the floor, exhausted over the subject. "Depends which one of us you ask."

"I thought I was asking *you.*"

He lifted his gaze to see his dad and brother waiting for his response like a blue-eyed firing squad. Matt shrugged. "We're still running into the same wall. She doesn't trust a word I say. Thinks I'll leave again."

"Wonder where she got that notion." Luke grunted low in his throat. "You've retired twice now, right? Who are you, Brett Favre? Just retire already."

Between his family and Jess, clearly everyone had conspired against him. "You know why I can't. It's complicated."

"How so?" his dad asked, shocking both sons when he piped in. "Just quit, Son. It's as easy as that."

Matt met his dad's level gaze. "Believe me, at this point I'd love to, Pop, but I can't. I accepted another assignment *before* I made my retirement official. Before I mentioned it to Max. It has to do with Jessie's shop and I can't get out of it. Luke knows about it."

His dad looked to Luke. "This about that loan you gave her?"

Luke frowned and nodded. "It's complicated."

"Matt said that already," Stern said. "And you look guilty. Why?"

"Because it wasn't my money that I loaned her," Luke said. "But she thinks it was."

"You're going to have to explain that one, Son."

"It was after Ken Dowry passed away," Luke said. "After she found out he'd given her the shop. I'd stopped by the house for Brody, but she was home early. Jessie never misses work so I had to ask. She'd just returned from the bank and seemed pretty upset, so of course I pressed her about it, and that's when she told me about the deli's urgent need for a new roof, paint and numerous appliances that hadn't worked properly in years. Never mind that horrible green furniture Dowry kept in the place. She'd applied for a loan but the bank had turned her down."

"I don't understand," Stern said. "I thought the deli was doing fine. At its worst, the place was popular. And since the changes—gosh, your mother and I can't go anywhere without hearing about one of Jessie's latest creations. The place is never empty. How could the bank turn her down?"

"The divorce," Matt said. "We were still finalizing. Funds were scattered or otherwise tied up. So one day I get this call from Luke…"

"So it *was* you," his dad said, passing that silent judgment over his reading glasses. "You gave her the money." Stern's gaze swung back to Luke. "Well that explains it. Your mother was wondering where you got that kind of money with the rehabilitation sucking up your savings."

Luke shook his head. "It's killing me to keep lying to her about it, too. She treats me like a partner in the business now. Bringing by spreadsheets with her payments. She's so responsible and trusting, and here I am lying to her face and depositing her payments into a college fund Matt set up for Brody. I'm eyeball deep in lies and I can't get out."

"But that's why I can't quit," Matt said. "The client—who's paranoid with good reason—specifically requested me for this job because we'd worked together in the past and he trusts me. I'd already planned to retire at the time. To get back to Violet Valley and get her back." He sagged to consider the work ahead of him with Jessie. "Or at least to be a better father to Brody. I even turned the client down the first time. But then Luke called and told me about Ken's death and Jessie's situation, and when the client came back with an offer of double the pay with a third upfront as a retainer, I couldn't say no." Matt rubbed his jaw. "So I can't get out of it now. We've already done part of the planning and the money I gave Jess is gone. I can't step away from this for convenience. I *do* intend to retire, but unfortunately, it'll have to be after this contract."

"Does Jessie know yet? That you're leaving again?" Luke asked.

"Not exactly."

"Mm." Their father sighed and lifted his paper. "Interesting day to find out I raised a couple of liars."

"This is different," Luke said, his face flush with embarrassment. "We're lying because we care about her."

"Poppycock," Stern said, ruffling his paper. "Jessie isn't a child."

Luke frowned and took a last swallow of his coffee, pulling his beige Resistol onto his head. He glanced through the window behind Matt. "Ah, daylight." He stood. "Pop has a point, Matt. You're walking a slippery slope trying to gain her trust while lying to her."

"I'm not lying to her," Matt said, watching his brother lean into his cane. "I simply haven't told her yet. There's a difference."

"Murky waters, my friend," Luke murmured, waving a hand in the air as he headed toward the mudroom. "Murky waters. Better keep an eye on that Cole McLeod while you're taking your time telling her the truth. I've seen his patrol car parked at the deli quite a bit lately. He's got a quickness to his step these days, if you know what I mean."

Matt scowled and turned to the window again. The sunrise had finally crept over the ridge, bringing the entire valley to life.

"He's a good guy," Luke said. "She could've picked worse, if they *are* seeing each other. You know. *That* way. Did you ever think maybe you should—"

"Shut it," Matt said, unable to hear another word about Cole McLeod.

Luke sighed, his distinct gait echoing over the hardwood until he disappeared into the mudroom.

Matt's fists stayed clenched long after the front door closed.

"Son."

He detected an edge in his dad's voice. "What?"

The paper rustled and he turned to see his dad studying him, the crinkled newspaper heaped in his lap. The old man's compassionate blue eyes softened his sun-weathered face and that stark contrast of salt and pepper hair. "I don't often tell a man his business, but you're aware that anything beginning with a lie can't end well, right?"

Matt turned back to the window and drank his last swallow of cold coffee. "Yeah. I know."

"You need to tell her about the loan," Stern said. "About the contract and why you can't back out of it. Give your wife a little credit."

"*Ex*-wife," Matt muttered, dropping his head and looking at several soap bubbles still popping on the bottom of the sink. Jess would lose her ever-loving mind when she found out he was behind the thirty grand she'd accepted from Luke to fix up the deli. His dad didn't know Jessie the way Matt did. He didn't have a clue about Jessie's pride. How stubborn she could be when it came to taking care of herself. Even worse, how mule-headed she was about that business she'd inherited from the old man, Ken Dowry, who had meant more to her than her own father.

"Oh, and Son?" His dad's newspaper made that rustling sound again, his voice sounding muffled behind the paper. "While you're at it, y'might want to tell Jessie you're still in love with her."

Matt's shoulders drooped and he sighed.

"Juuust something to think about," his dad said.

*****

"You want me to invite Matt to do *what?*" Jessie said into the phone.

"Just consider it," Terri said, sounding much too lucid for six-thirty in the morning. "It's bad enough Cole was there to muck up everything last night and now I have to contend with that. As if I needed another challenge."

"What are you talking about?"

"I'm saying," Terri said with a sigh, "that you can't mess this up by continuing the herculean task of doing everything on your own. Your condition isn't improving, my friend. It's time to let someone else carry the water. Look, I think this is one of those important precipices in your relationship. A big holy-cow opportunity and you can't screw it up. Let him into your life, for petesake."

"Cole? He's already in my life. As much as he can be."

"I'm talking about *Matt,* you dope," Terri said.

"We're divorced, Terri. I swear it's like nobody remembers that."

"The sooner you quit kidding yourself, the sooner I can fix this," Terri said, murmuring and sipping her coffee loudly, as though she couldn't stop talking long enough to take a drink. "But we'll talk about that when I see you at the festival Saturday. For now, let's focus on the daddy thing."

"What daddy thing?"

"It's time for a certain person to pull his weight in the parenting department. I mean, you need help with Brody in so many areas I can't list them all. It's high time someone else stepped up to the plate."

Jessie stared at a vase of flowers on the end table, unable to imagine her life without the brunt of her child's future resting on her shoulders.

"Jessie?"

"What?"

"That someone else would be Matt, by the way," Terri said. "In case you were curious."

Jessie shifted on the sofa. "I need someone in my life I can count on, Ter. Matt isn't that person anymore."

"Matt *wasn't* that person," Terri said, eating something now and talking with a full mouth. "Well, he was. And then he wasn't. But he's changed."

"How could you possibly know that?"

"Because he lost you, honey. You and Matt had been *you and Matt* for so many years that he couldn't possibly imagine a life without you, much less imagine you with anyone else. You were there to come home to. His lifeline. Now he's alone. He has nothing to tether him."

"I need more in my life than being someone's tether. Besides, he could be seeing someone else. He's as free and divorced as I am."

"Just because a piece of paper says your free doesn't mean you're free. He isn't any freer of you than you are of him." She paused for a long moment as if wanting to say more. "Besides, he's here in Violet Valley with *you* right now, isn't he? Want to know why? Because divorce changes a person. Makes them reevaluate. Prioritize. He's had to have realized by now that his life means nothing without you."

"Terri."

"What?"

"Please stop watching those romance movies or you'll be the one who needs a tether to reality."

Terri ignored the jab and continued as if Jessie hadn't interrupted. "The strain of Brody's issues has taken a toll on your health, and you can't keep pretending you have control over a situation that, in fact, has had control over you for a while now. Matt has two deliciously broad shoulders. Let him take this on. Brody needs him, and although you won't admit it, you need him, too."

Jessie pulled in a slow breath, brushing her fingertips over her lips as she remembered that incredible kiss last night that had nearly made her knees buckle. It had been a long time since Matt had kissed her like that.

"And don't take this wrong, but your childhood has seriously made you a bit of a control freak." Terri made a point to mention this at least once a year. "It's time you let Matt take over the controls for a while. You need to get yourself well and telling him the realities of being a fulltime parent to Brody won't be as effective as showing him. Tell him everything, Jessie. Then hand over the reins and let him see firsthand that you're not exaggerating. See how he responds."

Jessie heard the sound of a motor cutting off outside. "Um, he's here."

"Oooh, he's early. I love that. Okay, you can tell me all about it Saturday. I want a full report."

The door opened with a light knock and Matt's boots echoed on the hardwood floor.

"Gotta go, Ter."

She could hear her friend's reassuring smile in her voice. "It'll be okay."

She quit the call and stuffed the warm cell phone into her pocket, trying to appear casual as he rounded the corner and spotted her poised on the sofa. "You're early," she said.

His eyebrows crashed with one good look at her. Clearly, her extra effort with makeup this morning hadn't fixed her sleepless look. His gaze lowered, those wheels turning behind worried blue eyes.

"I thought I'd help wake Brody," he finally said, eyes lifting to her face. "I'm assuming he's still a bear in the morning."

She nodded. "But that's another perk of homeschooling—no bus to catch so he usually sleeps in longer." Her foot bounced in trepidation, waiting for him to make a critical remark about that.

"What?" he asked.

She shook her head, realizing the dread must have shown on her face. "Nothing. You can wake him."

He gave a curt nod, looking great in simple Levi's and a navy, button-down shirt that stretched perfectly over his muscular chest and wide shoulders. Heat crept into her cheeks for noticing, ever aware of him as he passed by her on his way to Brody's room.

"Matt?" She forced his name past her lips before she could talk herself out of this.

He stopped. Turned.

She felt his gaze on her shoulders, imagining those blue eyes intense as ever. "Brody has an appointment with his psychologist Saturday morning." She turned to see those eyes exactly as she'd imagined. Intense as all get out. "With everything going on, I could use your help with that. Would you mind?"

His frown turned into serious consideration. "You want me to take him to his appointment?"

She nodded. "It would be a huge help to me." Her heart pounded to admit it to herself, much less to him. "It's difficult to take time off from the shop every week for his appointments. Lucky for me, Dr. Simpson has Saturday appointments, and I'd hate Brody to miss his because my life is a little chaotic this week. Normally, I'd ask my sister to take over the shop, but she isn't always reliable and this Saturday we have the—"

"*Kelley* is working for you now?"

The disapproval in his voice didn't come as a surprise. "Yes, and please don't say what I know you're thinking. She needed a job. Her life is all over the place at present. Unfortunately, that means she's not very dependable."

"Now I get why you're working twelve-hour days. You've got the biggest flake in town working for you."

"She's not a flake."

He smirked and she looked down, all too aware of her sister's flakiness. "It's too much, Jess. You can't work twenty-four-seven. You'll drop."

"I won't drop. I have Sundays off," she offered in her defense. "Except when I have to keep the shop open for a catering job."

"Oh, you have a day off," he said. *Sometimes*. I feel so much better." He shook his head. "Maybe you should consider getting reliable help."

"Kelley needs some stability right now, Matt." She didn't want the conversation to spiral into the negative topic of her wild sister. Time to shift gears. "It really would help me out if you could take Brody Saturday morning. So can you?"

That half-grin finally curled one side of his mouth. "Think I'm qualified?"

"Well, you're his dad. You don't have to earn his trust and you can spot his antics a mile away." She warmed when those dimples deepened. "It's probably time you met Dr. Simpson, too."

He looked as uncomfortable about that as she felt. "Probably."

"I can give you a crash course in Brody 101, if you want."

A spark of surprise in his eyes told her she'd clearly taken him off guard. "I'd like that." He nodded toward the back room. "But give me a minute to wake the dead back here."

He disappeared and she remained seated, listening to Brody's sleepy voice, a murmured question from Matt, and then laughter from both of them. The sound of it brought a smile to her face as a quiet peace passed through her. Maybe Terri had been right. Maybe it was time. Standing quickly and walking to her office—a small area off the living room—she focused on the task of going through her filing cabinet and pulling out Brody's school history from the past six years, including the daycare information that went as far back as toddler years.

She was trying to fit everything into a soft briefcase when he walked up behind her, smelling great. "He didn't remember about breakfast."

"He barely remembers his own name this time of the morning," she said with a grin. "He was pretty tired last night, too."

"He's heading into the shower," he said. "So we have some time. How's his appetite without the medication? Better, I hope."

His concern made her chest ache. She'd missed having Brody's father around—someone who loved her son as much as she did. "He's eating everything these days," she said proudly. "You should probably expect to order side items." She handed him his shirt without fully looking at him. "From last night. You left it in the bathroom."

"Thanks." He stared at the garment in his hand, looking surprised that she'd washed, dried, and pressed it. "When did you get up this morning, anyway?"

"Early." She handed him a three-inch stack of papers. "And these are a few of his files."

"A *few?*" he asked, taking the handful.

"Brody's school records, IEP's, grades, etcetera. I've also included his records from the daycares since that's when the problems began."

"IEP's?" He peeled back several papers, scanning quickly.

"Individualized Education Program," she said. "Special Services required these each year. There's an academic section and another for behavioral issues. With each IEP, his teachers and I set new goals. You'll notice variations from year to year. He only received new goals when he'd met old goals. Many goals repeat from year to year, and a few he never overcame. The chronic lying, as you know.

We're still chipping away at that one."

He flipped through several pages and back to the first, scanning the top document quickly and with a frown.

"It's in chronological order. You'll see his progress and setbacks. I don't expect you to read all of this now. Take it with you for later. It's volumes to weed through, but it'll give you an idea of his real progress in school. Or lack of it. Part of that based-in-reality thing you mentioned last night," she added, then cleared her throat when she realized her voice had sounded playful and flirty.

That half-smile appeared.

"Um, Matt." She folded her hands together in a tight grip under her chin. "You should probably prepare yourself. Before you read this, I mean. I think you're going to find I haven't been completely honest with you about Brody."

He lost the smile. "Care to elaborate?"

"What I told you last night about his experience in public school was a rather sugarcoated version. I haven't been exactly forthcoming with the truth. I've been…hiding the severity of his disorder from you."

"Why?"

"Because I didn't want you to worry."

"I'm his father. I'm supposed to worry."

"True, but most fathers don't have your job." She looked down, ignoring the pull of that gaze. "The risks you take. I—I wanted your focus on the job. Not back here worrying about us."

"Ah, I get it," he said, teasing as his gaze traveled down a page. "No distractions. Don't want me getting anyone killed."

She couldn't be light about the subject that still plagued her daily. "Actually, I was selfishly preoccupied with you getting *yourself* killed."

The tremble in her voice pulled his gaze down to hers as an unfamiliar, almost gentle expression crossed his features. "So why show me all of this now?"

She swallowed. Wondered again if this was the right decision. If he'd leave again and all of this would turn out to be a monumental, deadly mistake. "You asked for a chance. I'm trying to give it to you. Besides, I can't ask you to understand the homeschooling decision I made without giving you an idea of how I came about it. It's important to me that we're on the same page with this. I'd like your support."

"I don't know what to say."

"Don't say anything," she said, acutely aware of how small her office seemed with him standing in it. He smelled amazing—a combination of aftershave and clean cotton—little things she shouldn't be noticing. She was meeting Cole for coffee within the hour to try to explain about last night, and she still had no idea what she was going to say. "Most everything you need to get up to speed should be here." She stuffed her hands into her pockets. "I think you'll find he's a good little writer. Has quite an imagination. Funny, too."

"Thank you," he said, turning back to the stack of documents and using a large rubber band to keep it secure. "I appreciate the vote of confidence."

She smiled, trying for neutral as the memory of that kiss pressed against her like a weight.

He studied her a moment. "You're welcome to come with us if you—"

"I'm ready!" Brody interrupted Matt as he bounded into her office, looking wild-eyed and ready. "Where are we going?"

She shook her head. "Thank you, but I have to open the shop."

Matt nodded, turning to Brody with a grin. "How about Duke's Place? If I recall, you couldn't resist their German pancake."

"Oh, man. Yeah! Awesome!" Brody practically salivated. She smiled to watch the two of them together. No way could Matt ever deny that kid. The likeness was uncanny.

"Don't get too excited," he said as he brushed a hand across Brody's head, unable to fix the damp, windblown bedhead look. "We have something to discuss."

"Like what?"

"Weren't you supposed to tell me about homeschooling?"

Brody's expression crumpled like paper. "Oh."

"Yeah," Matt said with a pointed look. *"Oh."*

An awkward silence lasted only seconds before Brody blew it off with a shrug and waved to her. "Bye, Mom. Race you to the truck, Dad!" He took off through the living room on a mad dash to the SUV.

She shook her head, sympathizing with Matt. Counseling sessions with their son usually ended with eager nods and promises the kid never kept. Restaurants, too, became a test in patience in how often one could tell a twelve-year-old to keep his voice down. He had issues with volume, another quirky symptom of Brody's Asperger's disorder.

He turned to follow Brody out when he paused at the door. "I almost forgot." He turned to her. "Luke asked me to bring Brody by the ranch around one o'clock. Said he needed his help with something."

"Like what?"

"He didn't say."

She shrugged. "It's okay with me, if that's what you're asking."

"He asked that you come as well."

Guilt swamped her, as usual. "I would but…I have to work."

"I know," he said, blue eyes searching hers, "but it seemed important that we both be there. Any chance you can get away for a while? Probably two hours, tops."

"It takes me forty-five minutes to get from the deli to the ranch, Matt." She bit down on her lower lip. "Tell him I'll try." She hesitated to make any promises. "If Kelley shows today."

At the mention of her sister, his smile faded and he turned to leave. They'd actually made progress this morning, but as usual, he left the conversation with a frown. She watched him go, holding her breath until the front door clicked closed behind him. "Oh, Terri," she said, putting her hand to her chest. "What have you gotten me into?"

CHAPTER FIVE

Matt looked up from his sitting position on Brody's mattress, watching his son's fingers fly over the keyboard as the kid finished a typing test. It was the first quiet moment he'd had all morning—apart from Brody's constant tapping on the keyboard. The boy had started talking as soon as he closed the door to his SUV, and hadn't stopped until he brought him back to make sure he completed his schoolwork.

"I type pretty fast, huh?" Brody said, not looking at him as he continued typing the paragraph.

"Faster than I do," Matt said truthfully.

Brody's eyes scanned the screen in front of him, never looking down. "Mom said I should try piano lessons."

He had no idea if his child had an aptitude for music or if he even wanted to play—alas, two more things to add to his father-fail list. "We can pay for lessons if you promise to practice. You know, if you want to do anything well, you have to—"

"Give it a hundred percent," Brody finished for him, repeating what he'd heard his dad and probably every one of the Brewer clan say repeatedly.

The software program beeped when he missed a letter.

Brody stalled before hitting two more keys incorrectly, which made the program beep twice more. He looked at the keyboard, scowled, then back up. Matt guessed that he'd lost his place on the screen because the kid hit frustration quickly and slapped his hand down, hard enough to detach a few keys.

"Don't hit the keyboard, Brody." His son turned and glared at him, as the tips of his ears turned red. Matt tried for something a little more encouraging. "Try not to get upset. You were doing fine."

"No, I screwed up." His son looked away, his cheeks as red as his ears now with embarrassment. "I'll ask Mom to reset the program and take it again later."

"Does she usually give you do-overs?"

Brody nodded. "She says the point is that I learn it."

He thought about that. "You do realize there will be areas in your life when you won't get do-overs. There's more to tests than checking your knowledge and skill. You have to practice staying calm and thinking clearly under pressure."

"But you were talking to me," Brody said, his tone defensive. "I couldn't focus because you were talking to me."

Matt frowned. "Take some accountability, kiddo. You started the conversation. If you can't talk and type simultaneously then don't do it."

Brody took a deep breath and let it out slowly, as though he were counting to ten.

Matt couldn't recall his son having such a temper regarding schoolwork, but then, he'd left most of the academics to Jessie since she had been the constant in their son's life and tended to take over in that department anyway. "Why don't you start your next lesson," he suggested, looking down at the paperwork again that listed this exact behavior as part of Brody's problems. Lying. Unreasonable lack of patience. Failure to take accountability. Blaming inanimate objects or others when scenarios didn't pan out as he wanted. Or the worst of it, that constant perfectionism the kid had apparently expected of himself from an early age. The list went on.

"I thought you had to help Grams and Gramps today."

Matt didn't look up from the paper as he continued reading. "If your grandmother ever hears you refer to her as *Grams,* hot steam is gonna blow out of her ears. You know that, don't you?" He looked up to catch Brody's dubious expression.

"Dad, that's only on cartoons. I'm not five."

"Where do you think people who write cartoons get their ideas?" Matt shook his head, looking down then to flip a page. "Hot steam. It happens when people go crazy. I'm telling you, someone somewhere called his grandmother *Grams* once, and that's what happened. Hot steam. Poof. All over. No more Grams."

Brody snorted, holding back a giggle.

"Oh, sure," Matt joked. "You laugh now, but I'm here to tell you that your grandmother will lose her mind if you call her that. I certainly don't want to be around on *that* day. Do you?" His gaze met Brody's and he smiled. "All joking aside, I wouldn't get into the habit of calling her that, buddy."

The boy shrugged. "I used to call her Grandmother like Mom said I should, but Uncle Luke told me last week she prefers Grams."

"Well, your Uncle Luke is special. He can get away with a lot more around your grandmother than the rest of us do."

Brody laughed. "Okay, I'll call her Grandmother again." He leaned forward, trying to get a glimpse at what his dad was reading. "Are you here all day?"

"Are you trying to get rid of me?"

"No."

"Is it possible there's a program on cable you're missing?" he asked, looking up from an IEP to find Brody staring at his socks, a telltale sign his guess had been right.

"No," the boy said.

"Is that true?"

Brody's expression turned resentful as he looked up. "Mom hides the remote and the cable cord when she's gone. I couldn't watch TV if I wanted to."

Seriously? That Jessie had to go to those lengths to keep Brody from watching television only showed the lengths their son would go to get what he wanted. Talk about dogged. "Kind of a shame she can't trust you."

"I never watch TV when she's gone," he said in his defense. "It's not my fault she doesn't trust me at home by myself. I didn't ask to be homeschooled."

Matt looked back at the paperwork in his hand, having already noted the numerous times the kid blamed all of his behavior on Jessie. She had good reason for her suspicious nature. No way could all of these teachers, school administrators, and psychologists be making this up. "What's your next lesson?"

"Math. Long division," he added with a sour look. "I hate math."

"Wait until you hit Algebra next year." His gaze dropped to the next psychological evaluation and stopped on a sentence about Jessie's illness. He frowned and read it a second time, hoping for some morsel of information.

"That's what Mom says. She says if I get behind in Algebra, I won't catch up."

"She's right," Matt said, shifting his focus back to his son. From what he'd read, the more abstract the subject, the more difficulty Brody had with understanding it. Variables would no doubt push the kid over the edge. "Take your time with Algebra. Most people take a while to get the hang of it."

Brody grinned at his father's faith in him but still seemed preoccupied with the papers in Matt's hand. "What are you reading, Dad?"

Matt's attention shifted between the paperwork and his son. Finally, he gave up and leaned forward, resting his elbows on his knees. "Why don't we finish our conversation from the restaurant?"

"What conversation?"

"The one where you dodged my question about why you lied to me. The basketball team? Your mom homeschooling you?"

The kid shrugged.

"Not this time, Brody," he said. "I want an answer. Why did you lie about making the team, and purposefully led me to believe you were attending Oak Field?"

Brody bit down on his lip. "I dunno. I wanted to make the basketball team. I wanted you to come to my games."

"Just because you *want* to be on the basketball team, doesn't mean you'll make the team. You have to have the skill. Everything takes practice. Do you even own a basketball?"

Brody frowned. "No. It didn't look hard. And Mr. Jansen said with my height I should be a basketball player, so I tried out."

"Height is only part of it. I was tall at your age and I never tried for the basketball team."

"Why?"

"Because I sucked at it."

Brody snorted again. "You did?"

Matt probably hadn't used the word *sucked* in over a decade. He had to admit it sounded funny coming out of his mouth. "I rarely played the game, so you bet I sucked at it. Big time."

"But you were good at football."

"If you had five brothers, two sisters and the multitude of cousins I have, you'd learn to grab the ball and run for your life, too." Brody grinned at that. "Tell you what," Matt said, standing and walking to the door. "I think my being here is distracting you. Why don't you do your math and whatever subject you have after that, and afterward we'll talk a bit more over a bologna sandwich. Come get me if you have questions."

"What will you be doing?"

Clearly, the kid didn't want to miss anything fun. "I'll be in the living room," he said. "Your mom gave me your school documentation from public school, and it's going to take time to look over all of it."

Brody's eyes widened. "I'm doing better now. You can ask her."

He could sympathize. At Brody's age, he didn't have the best grades either. "She already told me. In fact, she said you're doing *very* well," he added, earning a huge grin with the comment. He smiled with his son, although looking at his boy alone in his room, he had to ask one final question. "Brody, I'm happy that you like the new arrangement, but don't you get lonely here with your mom at work? Don't you miss your friends?"

Brody's cheeks turned pink. "I don't have any friends. Besides, Mom explains things better. I'd rather go to school here. You're not going to make me go back are you?"

The panic in his son's eyes made him consider his answer carefully. "Finish your work, Brody," he said. "Your Uncle Luke has something planned this afternoon and asked me to bring you to the ranch. He said he could use your help."

Brody's face perked up. "Really? With what?"

"Finish your work and we'll find out."

*****

Jessie was a task away from closing the shop for the afternoon—thanks to no-show Kelley—when Cole tapped twice on the large window before walking into the deli.

"Hey, Jessie." His rosy cheeks confirmed that the temperature had indeed dropped significantly in the last few hours. Closing the door behind him, he took several steps and smiled. "Wow, your coffee smells amazing. I'm completely addicted to it," he said, walking to the counter. "Sorry again about this morning. I hate it when we miss our morning coffee."

She smiled and looked down, pulling a strip of plastic wrap out of its box. "Me, too. How did the call go?"

"Fine."

"Nothing dangerous, I hope," she said, busying herself by covering a peach pie with the wrap and placing it into the refrigerated display case.

"Nope. Just teens causing trouble. I won't name any names." She smiled, appreciative of how often he went out of his way to put her mind at ease. All those long talks earlier in their relationship had paid off; there wasn't a bunch of mystery with Cole like there was with Matt. Cole was an honest, open book. Something she desperately needed.

He leaned over the glass to kiss her, but as her thoughts lingered on Matt, she turned her head, letting her cheek intercept the light brush of Cole's lips. He noticed the evasive maneuver with a smile and smoothed his thumb across her jaw before pulling back. She tried to return his smile. Cole McLeod was a good man. She didn't deserve him. Especially after that kiss last night.

She wished she could blame Matt. After all, he'd started the kiss. But then she'd kiss him back. Lord, how she'd kissed him back. It had been a mistake. A *big* fat mistake.

A big fat mistake she hadn't stopped thinking about all morning.

"I should probably ask what happened after I left last night," he said, as if reading her guilty mind. "But I'm not sure I'm up for it." He settled himself on a stool as he waited for her reaction. Probably expected her to say a few words to ease his mind, as he would have for her. But all she could do was hand him a coffee and brush crumbs off the counter with a hand, avoiding his gaze the entire time.

"Jessie?"

"Um—" She would never be okay with lying, but she couldn't bring herself to tell him the truth either. About Matt, that kiss, or her marriage that was supposed to be over yet seemed right around the corner wherever she went. She shrugged. "The usual. You know. He's Brody's dad."

"He's also your ex-husband, Jessie. You've been together since high school. Divorce or not, that's a massive habit to get over."

Habit. She'd called that kiss with Matt a habit.

Punching a register button, she distracted herself by reloading the register tape that didn't need reloading.

"Hey," he said, his voice unexpectedly gentle. "I realize you still care about him. I was married once, too. You can't turn that off on command."

"Still married," she whispered, glancing at him long enough to catch those eyes widening in surprise. She looked back to the register, wishing she'd kept the thought to herself.

"What does that mean?"

She sighed. "Marie passed away, Cole. Matt and I split because we couldn't make it work. There's no comparison. She was taken from you. In many ways you're still married."

"You're right. It isn't the same at all," he said. "Matt's still here, isn't he? Alive and well. And from the look on his face last night, he's still waiting for you to decide."

She ripped the paper and removed it, blinking quickly to push back the tears. "Decide what? We're divorced."

"My guess is he's waiting for you to change your mind about that." He leaned forward and settled his elbows on the glass case. "Look, I've known you for fifteen years, Jessie. I've known Matt even longer. I can tell when two people are done, and from what I witnessed last night, you're both far from it. Admit it. You're thinking about him, aren't you?"

"Who? *Matt?*"

His eyebrows arched, seeing right through her.

She'd managed to insert the paper and stopped abruptly. How could she tell him how she felt about Matt when she didn't know herself? "I guess. I don't know."

Her chin quivered with embarrassment to admit it and she looked down, covering her mouth with trembling fingers. When tears finally won and slipped over her lashes, she thrust her face into her hands to hide the emotions she could no longer control. "I don't know. I wish I knew but I don't."

"Hey, whoa," he said, quickly rounding the counter to gather her in his arms as she rubbed her eyes, feeling ridiculous.

"Just be honest with me," he prodded, brushing his hand over her back. "Tell me what you're thinking. How you feel. About him. About *me.*"

"I—" She sniffled and pressed her forehead under his chin. Cleared her throat to stop her voice from trembling. "I feel like I—" *Belong to someone else. I'm no longer free. I was never free. And I shouldn't have done this. I shouldn't be here with you. I'm so confused.* "I don't know."

"I didn't mean to make you cry," he whispered into her hair. "What did he say to you? I've never seen you this upset."

Wiping the tears from under her eyes, she stepped away, putting space between them, certain she resembled a blotchy wreck. "You heard him. He said he's back. *For good,* Cole." Saying it out loud and to someone else— saying it to *Cole*—seemed to make the words truer. "He's finally come home." She realized the slip and looked down. "To Violet Valley, I mean. For good."

She felt his gaze burn into her but she couldn't look at him. "You believe him?"

Her lip trembled to hear the hurt in his voice, to know she'd put it there. She wiped her eyes again and tried to get herself together. "He said he's come back for Brody. To be a fulltime presence in his life."

"And you really don't think this has anything to do with you?"

"No. I guess." She shook her head and sniffled, trying to forget that kiss and how good she'd felt in her ex-husband's arms. Two more tears dribbled down her cheeks and her shoulders sagged in defeat. "I don't know."

He took a step closer, brushing his hands over her shoulders. "Stop crying," he whispered, shaking his head and pulling her into his arms again. "Okay. Let's break this down. Say he's home permanently. Obviously, that's a good thing for Matt. For all the Brewers. And Brody will be walking on air. But what does that mean for you?"

She stepped back to stare into those hazel eyes filled with compassion she didn't deserve. "Relieved," she whispered, numb with peace to admit it. "I'd be so *relieved.*"

"That's all?"

She wiped her face and clutched her elbows, turning to pace behind the counter. "Isn't it enough? Isn't it enough that I'm so relieved I feel as though I'm having some kind of mental breakdown? My hands and legs have been shaking all day, Cole. I cry for no reason. Laugh at nothing. Mrs. Miles ordered a pound of turkey earlier and I laughed. Who laughs about a pound of turkey? I probably looked crazy, too. I'm going to scare away the customers." She turned to look at him. "Maybe I should call Brody's psychologist. He could examine my head, too. Maybe the years of strain have caused me to finally lose my mind."

"You haven't lost your mind." He said the words sweetly but she noticed his small step back. "But I don't think our relationship is helping matters either."

"What?" She shook her head. "Nothing could be further from the truth. You've changed my entire world over the last year, Cole. Brody adores spending time with you. And all those hours you've spent getting him better prepared to apply to the Junior Officer's Program in a few years? It's meant the world to him. To me. You can't suggest—"

"I told you last weekend I was falling in love with you," he said.

She rubbed her upper arms, wishing she could think of something appropriate to say. He'd lost his wife two years ago in a horrible car accident. Then Matt had moved out for good and left for a mission that would keep him away for four months. Weeks later, her pending divorce became common town knowledge, and then out of the blue, Ken had passed away. Somewhere in all of that, Cole had stopped in to check on her at the shop. Soon they began having coffee together just to keep each other in the sanity zone. And sometime over the last three months, things had changed between them. Going out became *going out*. They'd even kissed a few times. But last weekend when he told her he was falling in love with her—words she feared he hadn't truly been ready to say any more than she had been ready to hear—she'd smiled and kissed him goodnight. She hadn't been able to say much since.

"And again you can't respond," he said.

She clutched her elbows tighter.

"Look, Jessie, I can be as understanding as the next guy, but I'm nobody's second choice."

She took a small step forward. "You're not a second choice, Cole. It's not like that."

"Then how is it?" he asked. "Because your description of what's special between you and me wasn't about you and me at all. It was about Brody and me. And hey, I get that. He's a great kid, Jessie, and I love spending time with him. But you know what I didn't hear? I didn't hear how *you* felt about *me*, and I'm finally beginning to understand why. You have no idea how you feel about Matt, do you?"

She stared at the wall behind him, unable to meet that searching gaze.

"That's what I'm talking about," he said, his tone grim. "And until you have a bead on that, Jessie, there can be no you and me."

"Please don't walk away," she whispered. "Our friendship is too important to me. I don't know what I would have done without you over the last year, Cole. Please, just give me a second to think—"

"Friendship," he repeated the word she'd used, managing

a bleak smile before stepping forward, cupping her jaw and purposely placing a soft kiss on her cheek. "Decide, Jessie. That's all I'm asking. But I think you and I both know you already have."

*****

One hour, ample eye drops, and a full makeup refresh later, Jessie slowed her Corolla to a crawl where the ranch's long driveway transformed from asphalt to dirt. She tightened her grip on the steering wheel, navigating past the worst of the potholes and mud left from yesterday's downpour.

Luke knew her precarious work situation; he wouldn't have asked her to leave the shop today if it wasn't important. She only hoped whatever he had planned would be another step in the right direction for her son.

She could use a little good news about now.

When the ranch came into view, she scanned the property briefly for her ex-husband, wishing her heart would quit pounding like two sneakers knocking around in a clothes dryer.

Terri had been right. Divorcing Matt and cutting him completely out of her life had been her worst decision to date. The strain of worrying about him hadn't dissipated one iota, and she'd quickly discovered how much she'd counted on his trips home, however long or short. More than anything, she'd discovered how much she'd counted on his phone calls. Without the reassurance of his strong voice on the other end of the phone telling her he was okay, her anxiety had reached new heights while her health had plummeted to new lows.

Then he'd kissed her last night and knocked her entire world into another orbit. She hadn't expected to feel what she felt last night, or this morning for that matter, and now she didn't even know how to act around him. How could she feel this nervous about seeing her ex-husband, a man she'd known most of her life?

Ridiculous. She was being utterly ridiculous.

Licking her lips, she spotted him standing outside the indoor arena, his cell to his ear under his black Stetson as he waved her over. Looking up to the main house, she found it difficult to believe this was the same house from her childhood memories. After renovations, the two-story house now boasted eight windows across instead of four—mostly guest bedrooms—with its luxurious and rich combination of red brick, white trim, and four columns that gave the ranch a Southern mansion air. More additions included Tessa's Kitchen, the guest dining room, and a game room, among other amenities. She drove her car through the wrought-iron gate and parked in the main drive next to his SUV, pulling her coat around her as she stepped into the cold afternoon air. She made her way along the porch that wrapped around three sides of the house and took the stairs down, glaring then at the stretch of space between her and the arena. She began a slow and ginger walk through the mud with her navy pumps, cursing Luke silently under her breath.

Matt looked over and stuffed his cell in his coat, hurrying to her side and lifting her easily into his arms.

"Matt!" She wrapped her arms around his neck and tilted her toes up, preventing her shoes from falling into the mud.

"Oh come on, Ms. Practicality," he said, walking through the deeper mud while her legs bobbed. "A forty-dollar pair of shoes is worth putting up with me for ten seconds."

She shivered at his devious smile.

When they reached the arena, he lowered her feet to the ground and quickly gave her space.

"Thanks." Sensing that her cheeks had flushed crimson in the cold air, she examined the shoes he'd spared from the brunt of the mud. "Success. You saved them." She looked around, avoiding his gaze. "So what's all of this about?"

"I'll show you." He curled two fingers for her to walk

with him. "I think you're going to like what Luke has in mind." They walked into the arena where familiar scents of straw, hay and everything horse greeted her like a bittersweet assault of nostalgia.

She'd mounted her first horse here when she was thirteen. Stern, Matt's father, had taught her how.

When they reached the arena, Matt nodded toward a couple sitting on a bench with a blonde-haired child. They looked worried and anxious as they discussed something over the boy's head. Brody sat closer to the arena, nodding as Luke and another woman spoke to him separate from the others.

She looked up at Matt. "What are they doing with Brody?"

"They're giving him instructions for Robbie," he said. "Seems Luke's been busy becoming certified in equine-guided education. The woman with him is Gemma Burke. She's a speech language pathologist and is in charge of the program. She contacted the ranch months ago, which ultimately got Luke into his latest endeavor. He's been absorbed in all things hippotherapy for weeks. You know what a sponge he can be when he sets his mind to something."

"Hippotherapy?"

"Another term for physical therapy using horses."

"Okay…so no hippos," she said, watching her son nod at something Luke said.

Matt smiled and nodded to the couple by the bench, who remained engrossed in conversation as their child concentrated on a round, red ball in his hand. "I met the Johnsons before the pathologist arrived, along with their autistic son, Robbie. Gemma thinks the boy is a perfect candidate for hippotherapy. Although, the last time they were here, Robbie had a meltdown when they put the helmet on his head. Luke never even got him on the pony. But he hopes between the therapist's guidance and Brody's easy way with younger kids that we can help him. They're explaining to Brody now what he should and shouldn't do around Robbie."

"Like what?"

"Little direct eye contact. No touching. Shorter, repetitive sentences, that sort of thing."

Brody didn't have a great history with following instructions, but she knew he'd step up to the plate when it came to a younger child. He loved playing the big brother role and seemed drawn to teaching, although he loathed being a student himself.

Luke glanced over to Matt and Jessie with a smile before he waved them over. They joined the group and Luke made the introductions with Gemma, as Matt's cousin, Pete, along with a pretty wrangler Jessie didn't recognize—the ranch hands came and went too quickly to keep up with names—brought two saddled ponies into the arena.

Jessie liked Gemma immediately. She had soft hazel eyes and spoke to Brody respectfully and with a confident, compassionate tone that demanded the same courtesy in return. "To recap," she said to Brody, "all we need you to do this first time is to sit next to Robbie. Put your helmet on and let him see you do it. Then quietly mount the pony. Luke said you can ride very well, but I've asked your dad to lead your horse around the arena, okay? We're going to show Robbie what we want him to do with his mom and dad. Your dad will walk your pony by Robbie repeatedly. Robbie may or may not notice you, but we're hoping he will. Let him see you. Talk to him. You're his example today, okay?" She looked to Luke. "If Robbie has another episode, we'll have to put him in the saddle anyway. I've explained the plan to the Johnsons. Once Robbie is in the saddle, it's been my experience he'll be fine. We can quickly remove him if that isn't the case."

Luke nodded and patted Brody on the shoulder, who smiled eagerly, enjoying being a central part of a group.

"Remember to try to keep your voice steady and calm,"

Gemma said to Brody. "We're not trying to teach Robbie to ride a horse today. We're trying to guide him from his world of safety into ours. With your help, he might eventually see that our world isn't as scary as he might think. The pony is that bridge for him."

Brody looked to Jessie. "Is this okay with you, Mom?"

"Are you kidding? You've totally got this," she said, giving him a fist bump. "Can't wait to see."

He smiled broadly. "Cool." He looked to his dad. "I'm ready if you are."

Brody and Matt walked to the ramp and platform the younger riders used to mount as the new wrangler brought a pony over for Brody. Robbie's father brought Robbie to the platform and seated him next to Brody.

Feeling in the way, Jessie turned to the nearby bench where the boy's mother sat wringing her hands and took a seat next to her.

"Is that your son?" she asked Jessie.

"Brody," Jessie supplied with a nod. "He has Asperger's Syndrome. He has his share of difficulties but he's good with younger children. No worries there." She'd probably never lose her need to reassure other parents when it came to Brody. It had become a habit after years of apologizing for his chronic meltdowns and questionable antics.

"You're lucky," Robbie's mother said. "I understand that Asperger's is high functioning autism and it isn't easy, but I saw how he looked at you and your husband. He spoke to you." Her eyes watered as she turned to her son longingly. "I'd do anything to hear Robbie speak to me. Call me *Mom*. Even tell me *no.*" She frowned and wiped her teary eyes. "Oh, never mind me. He gave me a hug this morning. That's a good day. I should be grateful instead of complaining to a complete stranger."

Jessie's heart swelled with sympathy. She'd never considered how fortunate she was to experience things like speech and touch that she often took for granted. "I'm

Jessie, by the way," she said.

"Tanya," Robbie's mother said with a nod in the direction of Robbie's dad. "That's my husband, Brad."

"How long have you been working with hippotherapy?"

"This is our second trip," Tanya said. "We live outside Atlanta. This place isn't exactly down the road for us. But the drive is no problem. An easy sacrifice to make."

Jessie understood completely. "Luke has a knack with kids," she mentioned. "If anyone can help your son, it'll be him."

"He has an ease about him, doesn't he?" Tanya said. "He handled Robbie's tantrum so well last time. And I mean that kid went into full catastrophic meltdown mode." Tanya's gaze shifted from her husband back to Robbie. "I imagine most people would run screaming from the arena but he didn't." Tanya turned to watch Brody and Matt, then back to Luke. "Gemma said she's been working with Luke for months. She said the kids warm to him easily. Robbie hasn't yet, but he doesn't warm to anyone."

The smaller child still had a death grip on his red, plastic ball, twisting it repeatedly in his hands. His focus never wavered, oblivious to Brody, the ponies, and his father who stood next to him.

Luke handed Brody a blue helmet—her son's favorite color, then a red helmet to Robbie's father.

"No," Brody said, reaching out for the other helmet. "Give me the red one. Robbie can have the blue."

Jessie frowned, wondering what Brody was up to, but Brad only shrugged and traded helmets. Brody strapped the helmet onto his head and leaned down into Robbie's view before patting it loudly several times. It wasn't the smacking noise, but rather, the color of the helmet that seemed to grab Robbie's attention. The child stared briefly, transfixed on what looked to be half a red ball strapped to Brody's head.

"Smart," Tanya whispered.

Brody looked up. "Ready, Dad?"

Matt rubbed the gray-colored pony's nose and nodded as their son, like an old pro, stood on the platform until Matt brought the pony into proximity. Brody was too big for this mounting technique, but if his grin was anything to go by, it was obvious he loved showing off for Robbie.

"He's watching him," Tanya whispered to Jessie. "Look, Robbie's still watching him."

Matt proceeded to lead Brody's pony around the ring slowly, walking from one end of the arena and back. Luke spoke to Robbie as this continued, pointing to them periodically while Matt and Brody conversed in soft murmurs from across the arena. Brody laughed once—he had the most contagious laugh—pulling Robbie's attention back to him.

After Brad successfully affixed the blue helmet to his son's head without incident, Luke signaled Pete to bring Robbie's pony. Hooking his cane along the gate, Luke moved with that profound limp as he made his way to the other side of the pony. Jessie knew he could walk without the cane, but with a rod in his shin and four screws holding his leg together, walking solo—even for a brief amount of time—meant he'd suffer with pain and muscle cramps most of the night.

Robbie pulled away from Gemma's helping hand, folding himself into Brad's arms as his father attempted to transfer him to the pony.

When Robbie realized his father's intentions, he threw his head back, stiffening against Brad's hold before letting out a blood-curdling scream.

CHAPTER SIX

"Do it," Gemma instructed.

Fascinated, Matt halted Brody's pony nearby as they watched Brad move in one, rushed motion, plopping his son onto the saddle and holding him in place. Luke followed suit, securing the boy on the other side. Robbie belted out another scream and threw himself prone against the saddle. The boy's face turned as red as the ball clutched in his hand while his other hand dropped and pushed into the pony's mane. Startled by the texture of the horse's fur, Robbie's eyes widened and he jerked upright, looking as though he just now realized he was straddling a large animal.

"See Robbie?" Luke said, holding the boy's lower back with one hand, his other at Robbie's elbow. "You're a natural."

Robbie looked to Luke, making direct eye contact for the first time as if to say, "Who are you again?" This time, he clutched the red ball tighter to his chest and grabbed the saddle horn, balancing with the movement of the animal.

Tanya appeared at Brad's side. "Sorry, I don't want to be a distraction but I couldn't take the sidelines anymore."

"This is Butterscotch," Luke said to Robbie, gently guiding the boy's hand from the saddle horn and back through the mare's golden mane, lifting the strands between his fingers.

The boy's attention never left his own fingers. "Butters," Robbie repeated, a tranquil calm settling over his features.

"That's right," Luke said. "Butters. Butterscotch. He likes you, Robbie."

Butterscotch nickered, as if muttering agreement.

Robbie smiled and Brad inhaled sharply, his mouth turning down as he tried controlling tears.

"Hey, Dad," Brody said, loud enough for everyone to hear. "I think Robbie likes Butterscotch. Does that mean he can see us now?"

Matt looked at his son with new eyes, aware for the first time of how amazing a simple smile or the endearment *Dad* could be. Little things he'd never really considered before now.

"I think he at least sees Butterscotch," he told Brody with a smile. "Which is a good start. Let's keep doing this until your Uncle Luke tells us to stop."

"Kay."

Matt and Brody began again, their gazes constantly straying back to the child that kept one hand gripped around that ball as though it were his lifeline.

Matt glanced at Jessie, whose rapt attention focused on the boy and pony that Pete slowly began to lead around the arena while Brad and Luke held Robbie safely on the saddle.

One glance at Jessie's round eyes and strained expression brought back memories of old arguments they'd had over Brody. Arguments caused by Matt's refusal to admit Brody's world wasn't the same as theirs. In retrospect, he could see now that his son's world wasn't very different from Robbie's safer world.

Brody looked at Robbie as they passed again. "Good

job, Robbie," he said firmly, patting his pony and then his own chest as if trying to impart a sense of self to Robbie. "Butterscotch likes you."

This went on for over thirty minutes, with continued affirmations from everyone, yet the boy seemed oblivious of everything except the gentle cadence of the large animal beneath him.

Robbie's parents had worked together on this different path for their son, and Matt found himself envying them. He'd noticed several years ago the differences in Brody from other children, but he hadn't been able to let go of the idea that if they had tried hard enough, if *Jessie* had tried hard enough, they could teach Brody to do everything like other kids.

Nothing like a divorce to slap some sense into a cowboy's thick skull. Then after a good hard look at his son's academic and psychological profile today, he could see every place he'd gone wrong as a husband and father. He only wished his eyes had been this open ten years ago. He would have done things differently. He could have— *would* have—saved his marriage.

Luke's expression was starting to look pained as he limped alongside the pony while holding Robbie steady, pointing out different things in the arena with short, succinct sentences.

"There's Brody again," Luke said as they passed.

"Hi, Robbie," Brody said, still a little too loud as he waved dramatically. "Hi, Butterscotch."

Robbie turned to Brody this time, his mouth forming the shape of an o with what looked like recognition in his eyes.

Grinning, Luke nodded to Matt.

"Brody," Matt said, giving his son a nod of approval. "That was Luke's signal to hang it up." Matt brought the pony near the platform and Brody did a mock salute—a playful gesture he'd done since early childhood when he learned his father served in the military. Dismounting onto the platform, Brody waited on his knees for Robbie like a little caretaker.

The minute Robbie's pony stopped by the platform, the small child fussed.

"Maybe it's the sudden lack of movement," Brad suggested.

"Can we take him one more time around?" Tanya asked.

"Would you like to walk one more time, Robbie?" Luke asked.

The boy nodded with a jerk, still staring at his ball. "Walk," he repeated, moving his legs back and forth in a motion to show he'd like to move again.

"Really?" Brad asked, studying his son's expression. "You want to walk one more time?"

Robbie looked to his dad, making that precious but brief eye contact. "Walk."

The amazement on Brad's features to be communicating with his son tore Matt wide open. They were witnessing something special, and the miracle of it wasn't lost on anyone. Tanya had already broken down into a mess of tears. Even Stacy, the new wrangler, sniffled as she took the pony's lead from Matt. Gemma was standing on the sidelines, feverishly taking notes.

He looked to Jessie sitting on the bench, as much a watery mess as Tanya, and knew he had to be near her. Crossing the arena, he stopped in front of her and offered her a hand up. "You okay?"

She pulled a tissue out of her pocket and dabbed her nose, nodding. "It was nice of Luke to include Brody in this," she said, grabbing his hand and standing. He followed her gaze to Brody, who waited patiently for Robbie in his final trip around the arena. "He's so proud of himself. Look at him. Our son is beaming. I've never seen him this happy."

Brody removed his helmet, revealing safety-helmet-bedhead hair, if there was such a thing, with the dark layers falling every which way over his head.

"And this was only a tryout," he said, turning back to her. "A successful one, I think. Luke said if we're all agreeable, he'd love to have Brody two full afternoons every week. Not just late afternoon. Do you mind?"

"To help with the hippotherapy?" She grinned and nodded. "Are you kidding? I'd love it. What do *you* think?"

Happy to be included in the decision, he couldn't stop smiling. "It would be good for him since he can't participate in anything that resembles physical education or sports because of that competitive, perfectionist thing. Besides, helping Luke with the therapy will serve as an activity to test his social skills. Kind of a win-win, if you ask me."

She narrowed her eyes at him. "Okay, who are you and what did you do with my husband?"

He arched an eyebrow at her teasing.

She noticed her lapse and pink crept into her cheeks. "*Ex*-husband," she murmured, quickly looking away. "I meant to say ex…never mind."

He still couldn't get rid of the grin, especially having put that blush on her cheeks, something he seemed to be doing a lot lately. "Luke already has three children he's working with, not including Robbie. He'd like to begin scheduling all hippotherapy sessions for Tuesdays and Fridays to accommodate his other riding lessons."

"It's too much," she said, watching Brody wave to Robbie again. "Luke has done so much for us already. For me." Her gaze lifted back to his. "I hate that he has to break from the ranch every day to pick up Brody. But I can't get away consistently; I have a shop to run. And I still don't trust Brody riding his bike two miles there and back every day. He'd get distracted and lost and…I can't think about it."

"I can help with transportation."

She looked at him skeptically. "Since when?"

"I told you I'm here to stay, Jess," he said. "I want to

play an active role in Brody's everyday life and that includes school. In this case, transportation. If we're going to homeschool him, I insist on having a say. Besides, you said it yourself—we need to be on the same page regarding his education."

Her mouth turned up, almost resembling a smile. "Are you seriously agreeing with me on this?"

"I read the paperwork you gave me," he said, ignoring his rapid pulse to see her warmer, softer side.

"All of it?" she asked softly. "You read all of that in an afternoon?"

He nodded. "We have a lot to talk about, Jess."

She looked down. "I know."

"Hey, you guys!" Brody yelled, turning their attention to where everyone had gathered back at the platform. "Luke asked me to show Robbie how to brush down Butterscotch. Can I?"

Tanya held out her hands to Robbie, who only pulled away from her and flung himself against the saddle again, grabbing the horse's mane in his fingers. "Butters," he cooed.

"I'm glad I came today, but I should get back to the deli," Jessie told him. "Do you have this?"

"I can take him home, if that's what you mean," Matt said, nodding to Brody who immediately hopped off the platform.

"Thanks."

He didn't want this easiness between them to disappear. Pulling off his hat, his mouth went dry as he contemplated asking her to stay for dinner. "My parents would like time with him this afternoon." *Seriously bad start.* "Rather, Pop asked us to stay." *Getting worse.* "For supper. That is…if you don't mind." *That was terrible.*

"You don't have to ask, Matt." She actually giggled at him. "He's your son, too."

"I meant *you*…as well." He jabbed a booted toe at the ground between them, feeling as awkward as a teen.

She suddenly looked down, tongue-tied as she hesitated. "Oh. Well. I…can't."

And just like that. Crushed like a bug. "Let me guess," he said, not having to guess. "My mother." *Or could it be Mr. Eloquent, himself?* "Or is it me?"

A smile curled her mouth and she glanced at him shyly. "Neither. I have to get ready for the festival tomorrow. I have hours of work ahead of me. In fact—" she glanced at her watch, "—I really, *really* need to get going."

She turned on her way out and he followed her. "The festival?"

She laughed. "Are you kidding? The Violet Valley Winter Festival? Come on, Matt. You grew up here. Flyers are posted all over the city. Everyone in town is abuzz with excitement. How could you possibly forget?"

"Ah," he said, coming to a halt with her when they reached the heavily mudded area outside. *"That."* People. Questions. Handshakes. He cringed at the memory of the last one he attended before remembering his promise to Jessie that he'd changed. Thankfully, she'd been too busy eyeing the deep mud to notice his scowl.

"Yes, *that.*" She said with another laugh, glancing at her shoes. "Surely Tessa has a booth this year. She never misses it. I was hoping to grab a couple jars of her famous marmalade."

He pushed his hat back onto his head, a little surprised himself at how estranged he'd become from his own family and hometown. Had Jessie been right about him? He'd planned for months to come back. But what if he couldn't? What if he never managed to bridge that gap, that space between him and everyone else? "That would explain why Tessa nearly mowed me over this morning in a rush to get to the kitchen."

Jessie bent to roll up her dark slacks. "I can't imagine your sister's life. Cooking for the guests, and hands, *and* the entire city? The chaos of one town is enough for me, thanks." She straightened. "Actually, you know what might work better? I have no idea when I'll be home later. Would you mind keeping Brody tonight? Here at the ranch? That way you can take him straight to his appointment with Dr. Simpson at nine and bring him by the hall afterward. Terri and I have to get an early start setting up the booth anyway."

"Sure." He shrugged. "No problem."

She smirked. "Really?"

"Is that hard to believe?"

"A little bit, yes," she said. "I've never seen you volunteer to do something as crazy as come into town when it's in full swing. I could ask Terri to stop by the doctor's office after we set up, if you prefer."

"No need." He dreaded the unwanted attention but he was determined to show Jess he'd changed. That he could at least try. "Shouldn't be a problem. I'll drop him by."

"Okay. Great. Thanks."

They stared at each other briefly, awkwardly, before she looked back to the mud and pulled in a breath.

"You ready?" he said.

She'd been about to step into the muck when her glance shot back to him. "What? *Twice?* Matt. No! You don't need to—"

He bent and scooped her into his arms anyway, and she let out a sharp inhale.

"Matt! I said—"

"Shhh," he said, frowning and trying not to react to how light and frail she felt in his arms. "I'm trying to do something chivalrous here. It would be nice if you'd let me."

He slipped slightly on slick mud and she curled her arms tighter around his neck. "Chivalrous?" Her breath fell warm and light on his neck. "You shushed me. That's hardly chivalrous."

He chuckled, still navigating the muck. "I'm trying to focus on not taking a nose dive with you in my arms—as much as I'd like to see you covered in mud just once."

"I believe that," she muttered, a hint of amusement in her voice. "Still, I can't believe you shushed me. Who does that?"

"I do," he said softly. "At least with you. Just this once." She shifted in his arms, relaxing against him as her hand loosened on his coat to brush softly against his neck, causing a flood of sensations down his spine. When he reached the end of the mud, he waited before putting her down, wanting to hold her longer, to make sure this chemistry pulsing between them wasn't just a natural gravitation to body heat. "You've probably noticed, but your stubbornness doesn't always bring out my best side."

"I noticed." Her fingers brushed against his neck once more before she realized they'd reached their destination. Pink rose in her cheeks and she glanced away. "You can put me down now." He lowered her to the ground and she grabbed his coat briefly to steady herself. "Besides," she added, still clinging to his forearm as she brushed off her black work slacks, "you don't have a best side, remember?" She smoothed down her coat again before straightening. "And what do you mean by *my* stubbornness, anyway? You're no walk in the park, Matt Brewer."

A persistent smile tugged at his mouth as he tamped down the urge to kiss her again. "Admit it. You don't let anyone help you. *Ever.* Even me when we were married," he said, still getting used to the past tense when talking about their marriage. "You're independent to the point of aggravating."

Her eyes rounded. "I accept help. I just let you carry me hither and yon, didn't I?"

"More like twenty feet, and only because I forced you." He finally let go of a smile when she narrowed her eyes at him. "Name the last time you let anyone do something for you."

"Are you kidding?" she said. "All the time. I don't even have time to list them all."

"I'm only asking for one. It's okay. I'll wait."

Her frustration was obvious as her gaze shifted from the ground, her shoes, his coat, and back to his face. "Well, I accepted a loan from your brother, if you must know. That was a big holy-cow favor if there ever was one. One I can never fully repay."

He looked down, shocked that she'd admitted it. "Luke mentioned it."

The heightened blush in her cheeks only amplified her embarrassment to own to it. "It was difficult enough when Ken passed away last year. To think I was unemployed one week and find out the next that I owned the store." Her eyes watered as she shook her head. "Ken's death, his…*generosity* was so unexpected. I know you never liked him. With good reason. He wasn't the easiest person. Or nicest. To you especially when we were dating. But he was important to me."

She didn't have to explain. Kenneth Dowry had practically been a surrogate father to Jessie since she'd worked for him as a teen. He'd already been an old man when they were kids, and his feisty, negative ways only worsened with age. But curmudgeon or not, the man had been decent to Jessie. He'd also owned half the town when he'd passed away, and numerous people had been on the receiving end of his charity, with none more surprised than Jessie to discover that he'd left her Dowry's Deli.

"But then getting the place up to code fell on my shoulders," she continued. "The shop needed more repairs than I could afford. No way did I have that much money. And you and I were in the middle of…" Her voice drifted at the mention of the divorce.

"Actually, my family and I were discussing the improvements you made just this morning," he said. *Tell her.* "A new roof and A/C unit." *Before it's too late.* "A new freezer and extra refrigerator. Tile. Tables. Chairs." *Quit stalling with the dadgum inventory and tell her!* "Luke said the place looks amazing. You always did have a knack for decorating."

She smiled broadly. "I'm very happy with it. But I couldn't have done it without your brother's generosity. I'm so grateful."

If he had a conscience, he'd look away. But that rare smile of hers wouldn't let him. To know he was partially responsible for it warmed him to his core.

But his dad was right. This lie couldn't possibly end well. Still, for now, they were getting along. And for once they were on the same page when it came to Brody. If he told her he'd be leaving soon, especially the reason behind it—the loan and numerous lies he'd have to explain— she'd never forgive him.

"But you aren't mad," she said softly, her perfectly shaped eyebrows knitting together. "I've avoided telling you because I'd expected you to be angry about it."

"Angry about what? That you'd borrowed money from Luke to fix up the deli? You've wanted to own your own shop since I've known you, Jess. To have your shot at the American Dream." Her trusting gaze tore at him until he had to look away and kick lightly at the ground. "I wouldn't want anything to get in the way of that. Least of all money."

"Well, it was get a loan or have the place leveled," she said with a short laugh, pulling her dark hair behind her ear every time the wind blew it across her face. "You remember it. The place was coming down around our ears by the time he retired, and that was five years ago. As wealthy as he was, I think he'd overextended himself and couldn't keep up the maintenance on all of his properties. Not that I'm complaining." They were standing close together now, possibly out of sheer need to stay warm. Her hands had moved from fidgeting with her coat to fidgeting with his now, and clearly, she wasn't aware of it. Her fingers trembled, as did her voice as she continued. "I loathed getting into debt, truly, but if it meant I could fix up the place and get it right with the inspectors, to finally make Dowry's Deli what I've known it could be—"

Her voice halted when he brushed a long, soft fringe of hair from her eyes with the back of his fingers. She stared up at him with that watery gaze and visibly shivered. Was she cold? Or did she feel this, too?

"Jess—"

"I should go," she whispered, jerking her hands from his coat as it occurred to her what she'd been doing.

His breath came out in a foggy exhale before he took a step back, offering her a smile to make the exit easier. "Right. I don't want to keep you."

"It's not that."

"It's okay, Jess."

"It's just that I have hours of work ahead of me for this thing. I want Dowry's Deli to represent well."

"I'd forgotten how competitive this town gets for those Winter Fest blue ribbons."

"Yeah. It's crazy this time of year." She looked down. Back up. The gravel made a crunching sound when she took another step back. "Thanks for keeping Brody. I'm happy about today," she added. "That I could make it, I mean."

"Even though you're so far behind now you'll never catch up?"

"Right." Another step back. "So…I'm off to it." Turning quickly, she slipped into her car and the engine roared to life.

He smiled, watching her drive away and realizing for the first time in a long time that maybe what they'd once had wasn't completely gone. That maybe he could do something about the miserable life that lay ahead of him if he didn't get her back.

Of course, to do that meant he'd have to tell her the truth. Christmas at the latest.

Because that's when he'd have to leave again.

CHAPTER SEVEN

After baking four pies, three cheesecakes, and a multitude of holiday cookies, sugar free tarts, and gluten free pumpkin bars, she still hadn't stopped thinking about Matt.

Food. She needed to focus on the two items she had yet to make if she planned to represent well at the festival. Last year, Violet Valley had canceled the Winter Festival for the first time in thirty years. Her mentor and boss, Ken Dowry, had suffered an unexpected heart attack and passed away. Having owned a number of the stores in town and with no children or relatives to be found, his final wishes had made more than a handful of unsuspecting townsfolk new storeowners, including her. But his untimely death had practically rendered the town closed for three days as everyone mourned and processed what had happened. To plan for one of Violet Valley's biggest annual affairs only weeks down the road had been unthinkable.

This year would be the deli's first showing since Ken's passing, and she desperately wanted to make him proud.

Pushing six bread loaves into the massive oven, she set the timer and headed to the front of the store. She grabbed her glass of water, took a sip and promptly pulled herself onto the tall captain's chair behind the counter. Her legs felt weak, and as much as she'd love to blame her shakiness on exhaustion, she was all too aware of the truth. Unfortunately, she'd likely made her ex-husband aware of the truth, too. She'd been a trembling mess of nerves since that kiss on the porch. She'd managed to reassure herself that the lapse in judgment had more to do with working overtime than it did with any feelings she still had for her ex. But only a day later, she'd found herself staring up at him again, wishing like a love-struck teenager in hormone overload that he'd kiss her.

Thankfully, she'd snapped out of her little dreamland and regrouped before she'd made a fool of herself. But high-tailing it out of there hadn't stopped her from overanalyzing her reaction all the way back to town, and by the time she'd returned to the store, she'd found herself in the bathroom throwing water over her face as she struggled against a full-blown panic attack.

What's worse, she hadn't had an attack that severe in months.

Maybe there were too many reminders in Violet Valley to move forward successfully without him. Too many pleasant and difficult memories around each corner. Too many springs and autumns, summers and winters that she'd spent with him. She couldn't enter a single building without the past pulling her back. She couldn't have one conversation without someone asking after him—yet another constant reminder that she wasn't the only one worried that her husband might not return home.

Ex-husband.

It had to be natural then on a cold day such as this, to drift back to a better time the second those warm, familiar fingers touched her cheek. To long for another kiss like that one on the porch. To wish she could trust him again.

Pulling off her disposable gloves, she rubbed her eyes and moaned, desperate to wrap her head around this.

Everything was going too fast to know how she really felt. She should be worrying about Brody and the stimulation overload that always came with one of the town's festivals. She should be concerning herself with getting her delicate cheesecakes to the Dowry's Deli festival booth whole and not in pieces. And she should be stressing if Cole had written off their friendship because she certainly wouldn't blame him if he had.

What she *shouldn't* be doing is thinking about her ex-husband.

If only she could be certain he was telling the truth. That he wouldn't leave again. She could quell her nagging doubts. Maybe then, she could fully examine all of what was happening between them and entertain a possible future filled with family and continuity that she hadn't considered in years. But there was no way to know.

Or was there?

A glimmer of hope made her straighten. She had an *in* this time, didn't she? Odd that she hadn't considered it until now. *Luke.* Of course, Luke. He was the trustworthy guy any girl could count on. She trusted him even more than she trusted her best friend, Terri, who would do practically anything for her loved ones if she thought the end justified the means.

Slipping off the chair, she dove to the floor and pulled her purse from where she'd lodged it between an extra pair of practical shoes and a box of napkins. She dug for her phone, found it, and noticed a missed call and voicemail highlighting the display. She punched in her code and went to the text icon, finding Luke's latest text from several days ago. She typed, "I have to know." Send. "Is he back for good?" Send. "Please talk to me." Send.

Luke wouldn't need further clarification. Matt. *Always* Matt. Of course, Matt. They'd been each other's crushes throughout high school. When teen love had matured into a proposal and promises of forever, Matt's mother, Fiona, had fussed as only she could, and then promptly tried talking Matt out of marrying the town drunk's oldest daughter. But the woman's attempts at derailing their future together failed, and eventually, Fiona gave in and invited the entire town to their spring wedding—what turned out to be the social event of the season. It had all been overwhelming for Jessie's small-town frame of mind. She'd loved Matt with all her heart. Wanted nothing more than to be his wife and have his children. But becoming a Brewer had changed things for her. She'd gone from having an absent father and rebellious little sister to having a husband and more in-laws, family and friends than she could shake a stick at. The townsfolk of Violet Valley had also legitimized her residency by finally recognizing her as one of their own instead of one of Jasper Parker's tainted offspring. Unfortunately, that meant her private life would never be her own again.

Even after the divorce, Matt's presence followed her through the constant barrage of questions by townsfolk who refused to acknowledge they were no longer together. *Have you heard from Matt? Is he staying safe? When's he coming home? That boy of yours sure is the spittin' image of his dad. Tell him to be careful wherever he's at.*

She sighed. Stared at her phone. Waited for an answer.

Luke had taken a special interest in his nephew from the beginning, and with every trip Matt had taken, Luke had stepped in to be a constant male presence for Brody. Through all of it, the good and bad, she and Luke had grown tight and were as close now as any siblings were, even if she could no longer claim him as her brother-in-law.

She could tell by the display of ellipses that he was typing his response now, and she pushed a hand to her chest where her heart thudded, waiting for it.

"Sorry gorgeous," he replied. "That's a question for Matt."

She exhaled, deflated. That would be a *no*, wouldn't it? Luke would have said yes, if indeed yes had been the answer. Right? Because Matt staying home would be good news. The town that loved him could heave a collective sigh and his family would be shouting with glee in the streets. Wouldn't they?

She certainly wasn't hearing any gleeful shouts. But she did hear tapping.

She froze. Listened. When she heard it again, coming from the general direction of the door, she slowly rose from the floor to peer over the counter. Matt stood outside the shop's large window, and when he spotted her peeking over the counter, the sidewalk lamp caught his growing half-smile under his Stetson.

Her breath hitched in her throat and she resisted the urge to slowly lower herself back to the floor as if she hadn't seen him.

"Get it together, fool," she whispered, standing and trying for calm. Letting him into her quiet sanctuary would disrupt her already wavering peace of mind, but she didn't have a choice. It wasn't fair to let him freeze to death simply because she no longer knew how to act around her ex-husband. She crossed the shop floor, fingers trembling as she unlocked the door.

"Hey," he said, curling his hands in front of his mouth to blow a warm breath against them.

A freezing gust whipped in behind him, ruffling her hair. "Oh my goodness, get in here," she said, stepping back as he followed her into the warm shop. She closed the door and brushed the cold off her arms. "Are you trying to get hypothermia?" She caught a whiff of soap and spicy cologne and quickly spun on her heel toward the counter. "Let me get you a coffee."

"Thanks."

She glanced over her shoulder at him. "Is Brody okay?"

"He's great. I left after he fell asleep." She turned the corner in time to catch his gaze sweeping the room. He turned once, twice, catching the changes and detail since he'd last seen the place. "Wow, Jess. This is amazing. Luke wasn't exaggerating."

"Thanks." Heat crept into her neck and she chided herself for letting his compliment mean so much. She pulled a coffee filter from its box and went through the motions of making a fresh pot. "It's got to be close to midnight," she said, not looking at him. "What are you doing here?"

"My point exactly."

She pressed Start and turned to look at him while gripping the counter behind her. "What do you mean?"

He rubbed his tanned hands together, still trying to lose the chill. "I mean it's late. What are you still doing here?"

"I told you I had work to do. The festival."

"I figured out that much." He breathed in the scent of bread loaves baking. "Smells incredible, by the way."

"Thanks." *Again.* Heat swept into her cheeks this time and she turned, hopeful he couldn't see. "If you're checking on me, you could have just called."

"I did call. The house. The deli. Your cell. You didn't answer."

She looked to the shop's phone behind the counter and noticed the absence of a blinking light. "You didn't leave a voicemail."

"That's because I called your cell first. I figured more than one voicemail might come off a little stalkerish."

She resisted a smile, flattered that he'd thought twice about it. "Sorry, my phone was in my bag and I've been baking nonstop since I got here. I didn't hear it." Suddenly restless, she turned and busied herself with old catering tickets that didn't need organizing.

His boots clicked quietly against the tile as he walked toward her. "Home schooling Brody must agree with you."

Her defensiveness kicked in, making her next words sound sharp. "Why do you say that?"

He leaned that towering frame against the counter, elbows to the glass, exactly where Cole had stood that morning. Proof that her life was a serious mess. "Because past-Jessie used to worry about Brody nonstop. Your phone was never more than an arm's length away."

She glanced at him. *"Past*-Jessie?"

He shrugged. "You're a bit different now."

She frowned, not certain she liked the idea of being analyzed so closely, least of all by him. "Most of the time I have my phone with me. I wouldn't say I worry about him less," she said. "Just differently. Besides, I never worry when he's with you."

He stayed silent a moment. "I didn't know that."

A twinge of guilt stabbed at her. Of course he wouldn't know that; their constant fights where Brody was concerned would likely have negated any faith she had in him as a father. She stopped putting the order pads in a pile and dropped her hands. Silence drew out the moment. "Well, please don't keep me in suspense. Why did you call?"

"Brody was worried about you."

She sighed. "That kid worries way too much and too easily," she said, grabbing the glass cleaner and a paper towel. "If only I could turn his focus to his studies instead of my health. You reassured him I'm fine, of course."

"Of course."

His tone sounded doubtful, which meant he didn't believe she was fine any more than her son did. She squirted blue liquid onto the clean counter and began to wipe. "So why come all the way into town?"

"Because I was worried about you, too."

She let out a bitter, blunt laugh. "Well, welcome to the worry club." She regretted the words as quickly as they'd slipped out. His sudden arrival this week and uninvited concern about her health had worn her thin. But dredging up past hurts wasn't going to make this night go any easier. Or faster. She stopped wiping and glanced at him. "I guess what I meant to say is that you don't have to worry about me. This is Violet Valley, Matt. Aside from teens finding a little excitement four-bying or tearing through cornfields in the middle of the night—" he smiled at her mention of their own teen antics, "—nothing exciting happens here. In fact, I've always assumed the lack of action here was one of the reasons you left us so easily."

"Easily?" His smile faded. "I didn't leave you, Jess. What I do is a job. Like everyone else's."

"It's not like everyone else's and you know it. You do realize that the whole of Violet Valley thinks you're some kind of James Bond, don't you?"

He snorted, unamused. "You're exaggerating."

"I *wish* I were exaggerating, Matt. Seriously, the rest of us scrub floors, spray counters and bake bread in the middle of the night, hoping to snag blue ribbons at a small-town festival. Meanwhile, you're off in other countries playing bodyguard escort to high-ranking officials with enemies and contracts on their heads. You're obviously very good at, too," she added resentfully, "or Max wouldn't keep talking you out of retiring.

His mouth flattened into a line. "I make my own decisions, Jess."

"I know."

"Max didn't convince me to go back."

"No, you did that on your own." She glanced at him. Back to the glass cleaner in her hand. Bitter and unable to hide the fact. "I'm sure you couldn't help yourself."

"What do you expect me to say to that?"

"Nothing."

"My job," he said evenly, "is not an adventure for me. It's a paycheck. And despite what you think, I didn't choose the job over you."

Oh, were they really having this conversation? *Finally?* She plopped the glass cleaner onto the counter, facing him. "You didn't? That's funny, because I needed you here. If you would have asked me at any time, I would have told you that I needed you here. I was twenty, pregnant and scared, and I needed you here. *We* needed you here. But you didn't ask me how I felt. You enlisted. End of story."

"I would have been here if I could have," he said. "I wanted to be. But I chose a better living for us. One I couldn't make here in Violet Valley. Jeez, Jess, I swear sometimes it's like you don't remember how badly we were struggling to make ends meet."

"You didn't give *us* a chance. Between the both of us, we could have made it work. As a family. Other people do it." Remembered loneliness surfaced and her eyes shimmered with unshed tears. "It didn't have to end like this. That's on you." She grabbed the cleaner and paper towels and set both under the register with a thud.

"You were the one who asked for the divorce, Jess."

She refused to roll her eyes and cheapen the importance of their discussion. "One of us had to end the cycle."

"I did this for us. For *you*. Why can't you see that? Do I have to remind you how we found out about Brody?" he asked. "You were pregnant and exhausting yourself working fifty-hour weeks at minimum wage. You passed out, Jess. Do you have any idea what it was like getting that call from the hospital? To find out you were pregnant that way? And that was you working yourself to death for tuition and a mortgage."

"You were working the same amount of hours. *More.*"

"Now add a baby," he said, as if she hadn't interrupted. "There was no end in sight for us. Hell, we didn't even have medical insurance. I wanted more for my family than that. More for you. This *job,*" he said with a tap of his finger on the glass counter, "provided more."

"Yes, it provided more because you were in constant danger of losing your life every time you left us. How on earth did that become our best option?"

He let out an exhausted sigh and straightened, hands gripping the counter's edge. *"When* are we going to get past this?"

"Get past it? We've never addressed it." She bugged

her eyes at him. "So let's address it. Tell me, Matt. Who does that? Who enlists and doesn't consult his pregnant wife first? How did I end up with zero say about something this important in our lives?"

"Jess—"

"Just answer the question for once."

"I didn't ask you about enlisting because you wouldn't have agreed so I made the choice for both of us." The words seemed to tumble out of him as though someone had shot him with a truth serum and he couldn't help himself. Almost immediately, his eyes widened, as shocked as her, apparently, by the impromptu confession. He rolled his eyes and swore at himself under his breath.

"Thus started the beginning of the end," she whispered.

His gaze slid to hers. "It wasn't my shining moment as a husband, I realize, but I wasn't going to let you work yourself to death."

"You've got to be the only person I know, Matt, who can acknowledge a bad decision and defend it at the same time." The coffee maker gurgled, signaling the brew was ready. She grabbed a cup from the counter and slid it in front of him. "I'm sure all of this is very important, or *might* have been once upon a time, but now I have to get back to work." She poured his coffee and left for the kitchen.

He followed her. "I may not have been around to help with some of the burdens that came with Brody's issues," he said, "but can you blame me for following a military career when it provided everything we needed at the time? It was an immediate solution for the majority of our problems. Come on, Jess. You have to admit it was the right thing to do."

"I'm not admitting anything," she said over her shoulder. "And I really do have to finish my work." Grabbing a large, metal bowl, she opened the refrigerator and piled red onions, serrano chilies, limes, and cilantro into it. She pulled out a larger glass bowl full of washed tomatoes.

"I regret leaving you out of that decision," he said. "And I'm sorry. But I swear it wasn't because your feelings didn't matter to me. How you feel. What you think. It matters."

"If you want to continue talking to me," she said, "then I'm giving you a task." She straightened and turned to him, arms full. "Ken's famous Christmas salsa won't make itself."

He glanced at the baked goods piled on counters throughout the kitchen. "Wouldn't kill me to help. It *is* my fault you're here this late. I was the one who coerced you into closing shop to go to the ranch."

"Well, right now I'm blaming Kelley because she bailed on me again today and isn't here to defend herself." His mouth turned up a little at that. "But it's really Luke's fault," she said, tapping the fridge closed with her foot. "And as usual, I find it impossible to be mad at him. What he did with Brody today felt nothing short of a miracle. I wouldn't have missed seeing the elation on our son's face for the world. For once, he was in his element."

He made a move to help her as she juggled the items from one arm to another, but she shook her head and walked around him.

"I thought you were going to put me to work."

She spread everything out onto her favorite counter that served as one large, white cutting board. "That was my nice attempt at getting you to leave. I really do need to finish this, Matt. And I'm sorry to say it aloud, but you in a kitchen? Um, no."

"*I* cook," he said, grinning.

She put a hand to her hip. "Since when? *Past*-Matt couldn't find his way around a kitchen counter."

His smile widened. "Is that a jab at our marriage? Seriously?" His eyebrow arched. "Oh come on. Think about it. Why would I ever need to cook with a so obviously superior chef in the house?"

She tried not to let go of the smile that was threatening her resistance. "Compliments will get you nowhere with me."

"I remember." He smirked. "Just quit giving me a hard time and give me a task."

"Fine. Coat off." She nodded to the back. "Then wash your hands."

"Yes, ma'am." He took off his coat and slipped it over a hook next to hers. She eyed him warily as he rolled up his sleeves while making his way to the sink. He used soap and hot water as if going into surgery, as if—like her—he needed to focus on one little task to get him through this discussion. "How you felt mattered to me, Jess," he said, not turning to look at her while bringing up the earlier topic. "It still does."

She stared at those wide shoulders, unsure of the entire conversation. "Disposable gloves are next to you. We can't have gunshot residue in the salsa, now can we?"

He turned and dried his hands on a paper towel. "I forgot about this."

"What?"

"That you can stall a conversation like nobody's business." He did as she instructed though, pulling two clear, disposable gloves tightly over his hands and holding both up for her inspection. "Better?"

She placed a bowl of a dozen washed tomatoes in front of him and grabbed a long, serrated knife. "I need you to cut these like so." She began making quick, long horizontal cuts to the tomato, shifted the slices once to make an equal amount of horizontal cuts, and one more turn to dice diagonally until she had a pile of finely chopped tomato. She looked up at him. "We good?"

"Very good. One question though."

"What?"

"Can we cut into that bread as soon as it comes out of the oven? The smell of it is making my mouth water."

She grinned, her face heating until she had to look down from his gaze. "No." She handed him the knife. "Those are for the festival. I *do* try to make a profit around here. Now get to cutting."

"Yes, ma'am."

She busied herself on the other side of the counter with the peppers and cilantro, cutting and scooping into a bowl. Matt diced the tomatoes quickly, having clearly picked up a thing or two since he'd been away.

"I'd like to try something new," he said, not looking up from his task as he grabbed another tomato.

She cut into the onion, trying not to consider who might have taught him how to cook. "Like what? Mango salsa?"

"No. Not food." He grabbed another tomato, dicing quicker than a sous chef. "I was talking about us."

She stopped cutting. Swallowed. *Us.* "What do you mean?"

"Us. You and me." He grabbed another tomato. "Together."

She stared at him as he cut the tomato with that smile on his face as if his suggestion wouldn't completely turn her world upside down. "But we're divorced."

"Yeah. I remember," he said, sounding bitter as he diced and diced some more. "It's not every day your wife says that living with you has become *unbearable.* Kind of hard to forget."

"Matt—" Her chin trembled as tears blurred everything. She hated recalling that fight. What she'd said. How she'd said it. How it had ended. The word *divorce* coming out of her mouth and the *different* quiet that permeated the house after he'd left for good that night. A quiet she'd never grown accustomed to.

He looked up from his task to see her faltering. "Jess, it wasn't my intention to—"

"I'm sorry," she started, interrupting him with a quick shake of her head. "I'm sorry but I…can't go back to that." Her nose told her the bread was finished baking, and she turned, thankful for the distraction as she grabbed the oven mitts. The oven timer sounded then, loud and annoying before she clicked it off. She avoided his gaze, using her shoulder to wipe the corner of her eye while slipping on the mitts. She sniffled and opened the oven door to the delicious smells of herbs, toasted grain, and a touch of Heaven. Smiling, she carefully pulled out the two three-loaf pans, placing them on the wire racks next to the cooling bread bowls.

"Go back to what?" he asked.

Closing the door, she pulled off the mitts, still not ready to test her voice.

"Jess, it would be different this time." he said. "We're talking. *Really* talking. For the first time in years. Going backward wasn't what I meant. I don't want to go back any more than you do. I'm talking about going forward. Starting something new. We could—"

"No." Her eyes welled again and she finally turned to him, jabbing her finger in his direction. "You don't get to come in here," she said with another jab. "Way past the eleventh hour. And do this."

"Do what?"

"Don't you see that I *can't*—" she said, unable to finish as she swallowed past an emotional lump in her throat. She turned from him and wiped at her watering eyes.

"I didn't mean to…Jess—don't."

She lifted her gaze to see him toss his gloves on the counter before crossing the space between them. She pushed her hand up like a stop sign, halting him from putting his arms around her as she took a step back. "Don't. Matt. I don't need a hug. Or you being sweet and understanding. Or you being here at all. You don't get to do that."

"Do what?"

"You don't get to come back and have a conversation we should have had years ago. It doesn't work that way."

"I didn't realize there was a protocol," he said. "Maybe you could explain it."

"I mean it! Stop!" She wiped hard at her infernal tears with both hands. "Quit being so…so nice."

"What?"

"Look." That sharp, emotional lump expanded in her throat. "We're okay now." The words sounded strangled. Barely audible. Completely untrue. *"Separate* paths. It's what we decided." She looked down from that piercing blue gaze. "It's better this way. I don't want to dredge up the past anymore. I don't want to argue. I can't go back to that."

He stepped forward, cupping her cheek with a palm to pull her gaze to his. "I didn't come here tonight to argue, or win a conversation we never finished. I'm not out to hurt you, Jess. In any way. I'm only trying to figure out what happened in our marriage so we can figure out what's happening right now. Between us." His thumb stroked her cheek. "Because something's happening here. I'm not imagining it." He paused. "Am I?"

She looked down.

"But something's also holding you back," he said. "Is it McLeod? Some kind of loyalty you feel—"

"No." She let out a breath, teary, stuffed up and too exhausted to step away again. "No, it's not Cole. It's *you.*" Another sniffle and she looked down to the space between them, unwilling to let him see how much his nearness affected her. "And it's *me.* And…and the hundred reasons why we shouldn't be here like this. I didn't go through the last two years of hell, Matt, just to pick up where we left off." Her voice clogged with emotion, making continuing impossible. She shook her head.

He pulled her gaze up to his again, his thumb stroking her cheek. "I didn't mean to upset you."

She looked down. Closed her eyes tightly. Wished he'd just leave so she could sort this out on her own. Everything was easier on her own. "Then please go."

"I can't."

"Please," she whispered.

His hand brushed through her hair, his thumb lingering at her temple as tears dribbled over her lashes, making her feel more vulnerable than she could bear.

"Jess—" he said softly, and with both palms framing her face, he lowered his head, pulling her mouth up and into a kiss so gentle that her legs turned shaky as gelatin salad.

She lifted her hands to his wrists, not pulling him closer or pushing him away but bracing herself as he kissed her slowly and again. He felt so good. Warm and perfect. Soon she stepped closer, wanting more, wanting him with the same longing she'd felt earlier at the ranch. His hands traveled down her body, moving everywhere, pressing her backward, inch-by-inch, until she felt the wall behind her. His mouth coaxed, soft and inviting, breaking down all her reservations with tenderness and longing she didn't realize him capable of until now. Their tongues melded and danced, sensual and enticing. Her mind recalled vividly how it could be with him. How well he knew her. Every little pressure point.

She lifted her hand against his smooth jaw as they kissed longer, desire pulsing through every cell. His hand stroked her cheek as the other dropped to grip the fabric at her waist and pull her closer. She sucked in a breath. Wishing for more. Wanting to stop. Everything felt too fast. He'd leave. He always left. And she'd remain in Violet Valley wondering about him, staring at her phone daily, waiting at the end of an assignment with that crippling heart-in-her-throat sensation when another blackout period lasted days longer than it should.

He pulled away to drop kisses against her neck, his mouth moving hot and wet as her breath pumped in anticipation.

"We should stop," she whispered.

The protest slipped out of her mouth without a single

ounce of conviction, and when his mouth swept over hers again, she moaned, clutching his muscular arms as those strong lips immediately convinced her she was wrong. Her legs turned from gelatin to soft noodles as teen memories of him long buried churned awake. Of how he'd made her feel even at seventeen. Desired. Protected. Wanted.

She'd missed him since then. Not just the passion; in the worst of their marriage they'd still had that. It was *him*. The person she'd once trusted most. Her best friend. She'd missed him. And she didn't want to lose him again to some political battle in another part of the world. She wanted him here. Safe. Maybe she could let this happen. Believe him. They could start new like he said, and then…

That's a question for Matt.

Luke's last text to her broke through the fantasy like a splash of cold water in the face. She pressed her hands to his chest, pushing until she broke from the kiss. "We shouldn't. We can't. *I*…can't."

He stared down at her, his quick breaths matching hers. He hadn't moved away yet, making her ever wary of his proximity and unable to catch her breath. It was startling to realize how easily they'd convinced themselves. Had she learned nothing from the past? They'd always had this. Passion and touch. Unspoken words. How could she have fallen back into the habit so easily? Did she have no discipline at all when it came to this attraction?

Because that's all it was to him. Attraction. She wanted…no, *needed* more. She couldn't afford to do this. Luke hadn't been able to lie to her, which meant Matt was likely giving her half-truths again. Wanting what he was saying to be true didn't make it so. If she let him back into her life, then she'd have to be the one to watch him leave again.

And this time it would kill her.

"We can't *what?*" he whispered, bracing his forearm against the wall behind her. "Feel like this?"

She gave a quick nod. They weren't kissing. But he was

right there. Hovering in her space. And god help her, she liked it.

He lifted his palm to her jaw, stroking it softly with his thumb.

She stilled his movements with a hand, unable to think straight with all this touching. It was doing crazy things to her insides. She needed time away. To be rational. To put an end to the insanity. "I need time to think, Matt."

"Okay." He lowered his head as he shifted, his mouth close enough that it would have been easy to kiss him again. She came oh so close. "How much time?"

She shook her head. "I don't know. I just…can't think with all of this work ahead of me. And you here…it's distracting."

"Distracting?" He pulled in a slow breath and brushed his lips above her brow, straightening then. "I honestly didn't plan this, Jess. It wasn't my intention in coming over here tonight."

She nodded, not looking at him. "I know."

"But this didn't happen because of habit," he said. "That's not what this is."

She should keep her mouth shut. Not say another word. Let him leave and take all the memories and that sex appeal with him. But she had to know what he was thinking. "Then what is it?"

"It's what you said. It's me. And you. And *this*—what keeps happening between us that doesn't feel anything like two divorced people should feel." She couldn't deny it, but she refused to admit it, and after seconds of strained silence between them, he finally turned and crossed the room, grabbing his coat. "I need to get out of here and get some air before I say something I shouldn't."

She crossed her arms over her chest as he yanked on his coat and walked to the kitchen entrance. Her chest tightened to watch him leave like this. "I'm sorry."

He turned abruptly. "For *what* exactly?"

For asking him to dice tomatoes? No. She just felt the

need to apologize. She wanted things to be better between them. Friendship. Camaraderie. Like her relationship with Cole. Not this heartbreaking, hormonal, memory lane thing that kept happening. "I feel like I'm leading you on."

A muscle pulsed in his jaw and she regretted her choice of words in an instant.

"It's not…my intention," she added in a whisper.

"Leading me on?" He let out a grunt of disbelief, almost a laugh. "I really do need to get out of here before I say—" He shook his head. "Never mind. I'm leaving." He turned to go, took two steps, and with a smack of his hand against the doorframe, he stopped again, keeping his back to her as his grip turned his knuckles white. He dropped his head and released a heavy sigh. "You know, I could kill myself for giving you a divorce."

Her heart somersaulted. "What?"

He turned to her. Jaw set. Angry. "I made it easy for you. You were miserable. So was I. And neither of us knew how to fix it. But now we've made everything an even bigger mess. This entire situation is wrong."

"Matt—"

"But you know what isn't wrong? *This*. You and me. We're not over. We never were," he said. "Because I know you, Jess. I know what's in your heart. You wouldn't—no, you *couldn't*—be here with me if you felt anything even remotely romantic for Cole McLeod. Admit it. You're with him because he's safe."

She could only stare at him. Rebuttals gone. The truth out.

"You want time to think?" he said. "Fine. You've got it. But this conversation?" His finger pivoted between them. "It's not over by a long shot."

And then he was gone.

After the shop's front door closed, she let out a shaky breath and numbly went back to the task of mixing the salsa as if he'd never stopped by. She needed to forget about her personal life for a while and focus on work, on getting the food prepared for transportation in the morning.

An hour past midnight, she finally slipped on her coat and stood by the door when she noticed his cold coffee still on the counter. She stared at the cup as she pulled her phone out of her pocket to see the voicemail message he'd left earlier before stopping by.

Clicking play like a person without sense in her head, she listened to his voice, warm and full of concern play back for her. He was worried. Didn't want her to work too hard. Would she please call? Could they talk later? Maybe over dinner. Maybe she'd let him cook.

With trembling fingers, she shut off the voicemail and managed to find Terri's latest text about the festival through a blur of tears, replying with a simple. "About Matt. Help."

Seconds after she got into her car and headed for home, the ring tone *It's Raining Men* sounded on the seat next to her, indicating a call from Terri.

CHAPTER EIGHT

Matt signed the receipt, pushed it under the glass, and found a seat next to Brody in the small office lobby, ignoring the receptionist's stare from behind the glass. He probably should recognize her from somewhere but he didn't, and he wasn't sure he wanted to. She kept staring at him as if he were a ghost. Gave him the creeps.

"I can't wait for today," Brody said loudly, knees bouncing.

Matt motioned a shushing finger to his mouth out of habit, reminding the kid to watch the volume. "Your mom said you're helping her today," he said quietly, as if others were waiting in the psychologist's office on a Saturday morning. Perhaps on a normal Saturday, there might have been other patients. But today was the festival. Nothing normal about that.

"I'm running the fishing booth," Brody said smugly, reminding him of Fiona Brewer for the briefest of moments. "I run it each year."

"Fishing booth?" Maybe Matt hadn't heard him right. "What does fishing have to do with Christmas?"

"Fishing for Christmas presents," Brody said matter-of-factly. "Aside from Santa, it's the most popular booth.

Didn't they have that when you were a kid?"

"I think I would remember fishing." He recalled too many sweets, running around with his brothers and friends, and getting into trouble. "Must be new."

"You should come today, Dad." Those knees were bouncing like crazy now. "You can watch me work. I'm good at it."

Matt would rather have a root canal than go to the Winter Festival with the entire town flooding around him like bees. But if Brody wanted him there, he'd be there. Besides, he had to show Jessie he could be different now. A man she could count on. A man she could make new memories with. A man who didn't want to recoil every time someone shook his hand and thanked him for his service to their country.

Dr. Simpson opened his office door, still murmuring to an older woman who held a tissue to her nose, sniffling and hugging him before she left in tears.

Matt stared at the door she closed behind her, shaking his head. He didn't belong in a shrink's office. Hell, he already felt psychoanalyzed simply by association. How could Jessie think for two seconds that he could do this?

Brody bolted from his seat as the doctor came forward.

"Brody, my man," Dr. Simpson said, lifting his hand to accept the kid's high-five. "Nice to see you again. Go ahead and head back—" Brody didn't wait for him to finish as he took off down the hallway.

Matt stood and extended his hand. "Matt Brewer." The older man had a firm grip. A good start. "Brody's dad."

"I'm glad to finally meet you. I can always tell when you're back for a visit because Brody talks about nothing else. And of course, Jessie has nothing but high praise for you."

Jessie must have lied. "Oh?"

"Your relationship with your son. Your wife said you're very close."

"Oh, we're not—" Matt stopped midsentence; there

was no point in correcting the slip on his marital status since he had every intention to rectify it. "Never mind."

A large thump sounded from the doc's office and Simpson looked over his shoulder, smiling. "Did Jessie tell you how this works? I usually chat with Brody for forty minutes or so, and then you and I will talk for the remainder of the hour."

"Sure. That works." The doctor left to go do whatever it was he did all day, and Matt grabbed a magazine that smelled of godawful department store perfume, flipping through the pages then as he waited for a text or call from Jessie. He assumed she'd worry how the session was going, but as five minutes rolled into fifteen, he figured she had her hands full setting up for the festival. That or she really meant it when she said she never worried about Brody when they were together.

"Your turn!"

Matt looked up from the magazine as his son bounded across the room like an excited eight-year-old. Matt and the receptionist exchanged curious glances before he checked his watch. "You were only in there for fifteen minutes."

Brody shrugged. "I told him school was going well and that I want to get to the festival before they open the fishing booth. So he said he'll talk to you now."

"Can he do that? Cut your session short?"

"It's his office, Dad. He can do anything he wants."

Matt nodded and stood, dry-mouthed as he made his way down the hall and into the quiet office.

Simpson sat in a chair, pad and pencil in his hand. "Have a seat, Mr. Brewer. Any seat is fine."

Matt eyed a couch and four seats, immediately deciding on a chair opposite the doc. The cushion squeaked when he sat, and he crossed his ankle over his knee, quickly reaching a level of discomfort he never thought possible outside of a warzone.

"Brody said he's doing well with his studies," Simpson

said with a brief smile. "He seems very energetic and genuinely positive about learning now."

Matt noted the word *genuinely* and recalled what he'd read about his son only yesterday morning—that the kid lied on a regular basis to almost everyone, making it difficult to discern how he truly felt about anything.

"I understand your job keeps you away for large amounts of time, Mr. Brewer," Simpson said, crossing one knee over the other, "but I was hoping you could tell me if you've noticed any changes in his behavior since Jessie started home schooling him—positive or negative."

Changes? In Brody? Matt pulled in a breath and held it, drawing a blank. "Um, he likes the flexibility of his schedule."

Simpson scribbled on his yellow pad. "How so?"

It was difficult not to feel judged by this complete stranger. Was this how Jessie felt on a regular basis? "He can sleep in, for one. He was never much of a morning person."

Simpson laughed. "Neither am I." More writing. "What else?"

Matt wanted desperately to defer to Jessie, as he would have in the past. But the divorce had left him a single father who had no real knowledge of his son's true personality. Coming to terms with that humiliating and painful realization, especially in a small, creepy office with the doctor looking on, wasn't exactly setting well with him either. Oh sure, he could recite the symptoms of his son's disorder. Details he'd read in the IEPs yesterday or tidbits Jessie had mentioned in conversation over the years. He knew from the kid's own mouth that his son didn't have any friends. Knew from observation that the boy could talk nonstop about practically anything. That he loved video games, probably because he didn't have to interact with people when playing. His son truly loathed math, enough that he used the word *math* regularly to relay how much he hated something. Like he hated cleaning his room…like *math*. The kid loved anything sweet, which Jess never allowed much of because he was already bouncing off the walls most of the time. But Matt would venture a guess these were things Simpson already knew.

"Did he mention what happened at the ranch yesterday?" Matt asked.

"I know he loves spending time there." Simpson gave Matt his full attention now, curious. "Something special happened?"

Matt, grateful now more than ever that he'd witnessed what amounted to a real breakthrough for his son, explained in detail what had happened with the boy, Robbie, and Brody's excitement at playing such a key role in Robbie's progress. They talked at length about the experience, and later, about what Matt and Jessie could focus on in future sessions to help Brody improve his social skills as well.

"The Asperger's has affected Brody's maturity level profoundly," Simpson explained, "which is why he does so well with smaller children. I'm glad you both found this option."

"It was my brother's idea, actually."

"His Uncle Luke?"

"Right."

"He talks about him often."

Matt smiled. Years ago when it was obvious Luke intended to stay at the ranch, Matt had asked him to watch over his family when he was away on assignment, which Luke had done faithfully and without question or complaint. Matt owed his brother more than he could ever repay.

"I have to tell you, Mr. Brewer, that when Jessie first mentioned the idea of home schooling, I worried about removing Brody entirely from children his age. And it's still my opinion that our biggest concern needs to be socializing. Perhaps now that she has a handle on his schoolwork, we can turn the focus back to his social skills."

"Actually, I'm more concerned about the lying," Matt said. "He lies even when he hasn't done anything wrong. That doesn't make sense to me."

"His perceptual reasoning is very high," Simpson said, "which, as far as I've observed, seems to be what leads to the constant manipulation."

Matt had read that comment twice yesterday and still didn't fully understand. "I don't follow."

"Your son notices everything." Simpson's hopeful smile flattened into a thin line. "Unfortunately, in Brody's case, he only seems interested in utilizing this eye for detail to better manipulate his way through life. Lying is a coping mechanism. He doesn't understand social cues. In his own way, he's been pretending his entire life. Lying to create a world he understands. And in Brody's case, he's created a world where he can be the hero of the story."

Matt frowned. "But that reality doesn't exist."

"It does for Brody, and he will continue to create that world until he learns to cope in this one."

Not unlike Robbie. Matt's neck muscles bunched painfully and he frowned, the weight of his son's future success and happiness residing on his shoulders like a 500-pound weight.

"I know." Simpson let go a sigh of sympathy. "It can be difficult. But perhaps now that you're home permanently, Brody will have more continuity in his life." Matt arched an eyebrow, having said nothing about staying. "I apologize," the doctor said, quickly clarifying, "he said you were home permanently. It's almost all he could talk about today. He worries about you and his mother quite a bit."

"About that." Matt shifted, uneasy. "He's excessively worried about Jessie. To an unhealthy degree. I realize her health is an issue right now, but is that normal for a child to obsess like that?"

"In this case, yes. You have to remember that Brody's

mom is the center of his world. The one constant." Simpson frowned and placed the notepad on the chair's arm. "But the stress of raising Brody has taken a toll on her health, and she can no longer hide that fact from him."

"I'm hoping to change that."

Simpson studied him for a moment, looking skeptical. "Mr. Brewer, it's important to mention that even in a stable home with two fulltime, loving parents, a child with Asperger's can pose an ongoing daily challenge. It can sometimes be a bit of a…wearing-down process. Jessie has essentially been a single parent to a boy who—well, your son is very special. Comparatively speaking, he's the equivalent of five children. I've told Jessie this repeatedly when she expects too much of herself. Sometimes raising a child with high-functioning autism is an even bigger battle than raising a child with a physical disability that everyone can see."

The comparison startled Matt. "How's that?"

Simpson shrugged. "Most people feel if they've watched the movie *Rain Man* that they have an understanding of autism. What they don't understand is that each autistic child or adult—high functioning or otherwise—is a unique individual with different needs, like everyone else. But it's easier to put people into molds. I'd go so far as to put it this way—and it's not a very charitable thing for me to say—but Jessie has been fighting an uphill battle with an ignorant community and an unfortunate amount of well-meaning friends and family. For every step she takes forward, she has to take three back, simply to indulge people who need to believe that the world is flat. Fighting this battle on a daily basis has been a wearing down process for her. A bit of a…*slow-drip* decline into depression. That Jessie has handled it this well for this long says a lot about her strength of character."

Matt swallowed, unable to deny his pivotal role in that decline.

"It's easy to be critical of a parent with Brody's issues,"

he continued. "Especially in a close-knit community such as Violet Valley. Everyone considers themselves family and *everyone* has an opinion."

"I didn't know it was this bad for her," Matt said. "She never asked for help." Not that he'd given her a chance. "I'm not blaming her. She had her reasons."

"She did," Simpson confirmed. "But now that you'll be around permanently, you won't need Jessie to explain anything. You'll be here to observe all of this firsthand."

"I have every intention to make up for lost time. I want to take the brunt of this off her, at least until she's healthy again."

"Continuity is essential with Brody. I would advise any changes be introduced gradually and consistently."

More judgment. "I can't say there won't be upsets in the new schedule, especially in the beginning." He didn't want to mention leaving after Christmas since he could do nothing about the fact. "I understand about Brody's need for continuity. But Jessie's health…it has to be a priority right now."

Simpson rubbed his jaw. "Yes, the effects of the PTSD," he said. "It's an unfortunate consequence of the sustained stress."

Matt tried to keep his expression neutral as if her diagnosis wasn't news to him. Post-Traumatic Stress Disorder. How could that be? He rubbed the back of his neck where the muscles knotted tighter. PTSD? Jessie? His Jessie? Why hadn't she said anything? How could he have missed the signs?

"Is she sleeping better?" Simpson asked.

"Not really." The dark circles under her eyes would make that obvious to anyone.

"That'll come in time, I think," Simpson said. "Home schooling Brody seems to have helped her get a bit of control back into her life. She had more color and energy the last time we spoke. She seemed more at peace."

And Matt had almost taken that from her as well. Now

more than ever, he understood her fierce reaction to his suggestion that Brody go back to public school.

A knock sounded and Brody poked his head in the door. "Dad, they're probably opening the fishing booth without me."

"Brody," Simpson said, "we're not done with your session. Please wait in the lobby until we're finished."

"Sorry, Dr. Simpson," Brody said, shifting restlessly and looking to Matt. "Is it okay, Dad? Just this once? I don't want them starting without me."

Matt stood, ideas rushing forward as he felt the same need to get out of the office and find Jessie. To sort their lives out once and for all. How had she been the one between them to end up with PTSD?

He held out a hand to Simpson again. "Sorry. He's excited and…I have things to do as well that can't wait." First and foremost, find Jessie. Then his brother, Sam, to discuss their possible new venture together.

Simpson stood and accepted his handshake. "Of course. I get it." He glanced to Brody. "Practice those calming techniques, okay?"

"Yep," Brody said, nodding dramatically. He turned back to Matt. "Let's go Dad. We should hurry."

"I plan to stop by the festival as well," Simpson said, looking between them. "And if I don't see you there, perhaps both you and Jessie will drop by for Brody's next appointment. Say, after Christmas?"

Matt's heart sank like a stone. Even with all of his desire to do the right thing by Jessie and his son, to repair what had broken between them, he still wasn't free to fully commit to it.

And he wouldn't be for months.

*****

"Hells bells," Terri sang out, looking at the hall entrance.

"She said *jingle bells*," Jessie said to the elderly and hard-of-hearing Mrs. Thompson, before grabbing a paper soup cup and giving Terri a light elbow jab.

Terri smiled at Mrs. Thompson, following up with a mischievous grin at Jessie. Terri looked comical wearing that goofy, straw hat with the mistletoe tied to the brim. "You won't believe who just walked in."

"Let me guess." Jessie stirred the chili. "Santa."

"Not. Even. Close. But I'll bet he looks smashing in red. I'll give you a hint. *Serious* eye candy."

Jessie checked the heating element. "I'm more concerned about these beans burning than eye candy right now, Ter."

"*And* he's tall. Gorgeous. Brought your son, who happens to look an awful lot like him, by the way."

"You're so transparent, Terri," Jessie muttered, ladling hot chili into the bowl. Too many people milled around the town's Great Hall for Jessie to look up and confirm that her husband had indeed arrived. She turned and handed the bowl to Mrs. Thompson as Terri continued to watch Jessie for a reaction.

When Mrs. Thompson disappeared to look for a table, Jessie peered through the crowd and quickly spotted Matt by the main door. He was difficult to miss—towering over most everyone and extremely easy on the eyes.

Brody stood next to him, impatiently waiting for his dad, who couldn't extract himself from the entrance while one resident after another approached him, shaking his hand dramatically while patting his arm. More appreciation for serving his country, no doubt.

Terri passed a fresh loaf of dill bread and an apple spice tart to a customer in exchange for a check. "That's a full two minutes he's been standing there. They won't let your poor hubby through the door."

"*Ex*-hubby, Ter." Jessie watched him smile and say the right things, forever the humble and faithful soldier, long after his military service had ended.

"Nothing as sexy as a cowboy in a Stetson," Terri said.

"Please," Jessie said, trying to derail her friend. "He

hasn't worked a ranch in years. Not in that way, anyway."

"Doesn't matter. The man is seriously yummy. You can't bother to deny it. Your face is turning red just thinking about that hot bod. Admit it."

Jessie didn't want to admit anything. Especially the reason her cheeks were overheating. The notion of doing anything with Matt these days made her blush. When was this divorce supposed to kick in and remind her she shouldn't feel like this about him? Yesterday. Last night. It would have been all too easy to…

"I said *two* potato soups, dear," Mrs. Bowersox said, holding up two fingers in front of Jessie's nose.

"Sorry. Cup or bread bowl?"

"Two bread bowls please."

She recalled the woman asking for bread bowls once already. Jessie shook her head, trying to get her mind back into the game as she reached behind her for two bread bowls. Watching her ex attempt to untangle himself from the never-ending Matt Brewer fan club made her cringe for him. He hated the attention. But he also understood the good intentions behind the fanfare, which meant he would never be anything less than cordial and grateful.

Brody scowled as another person stopped Matt a foot from the door. Jessie caught her son's attention and waved him over. He was pink-cheeked by the time he reached her. "Did they start?"

"Are you kidding?" She pulled out a free cookie for the five-year-old Tammy Lynn Jones, who stood on tiptoes, eyes just above the counter as her fingers grabbed for anything sweet. "Look at the line over there. They're all waiting for you."

Brody looked over to the twenty-plus children of various ages waiting for the fishing booth to open. "I've totally got this," he said with a grin and took off for the booth.

"That kid *loves* being in charge of that booth," Terri said after Brody left.

"Can't blame him." Jessie looked back to Matt, who had made it an entire six feet into the hall and was now talking to Mr. Jacoby, one of their teachers from high school. "He struggles with so many things in his life. I wouldn't begrudge him this one day a year when he can shine."

"Be still my heart," Terri said, looking back to the door. "Another Brewer boy and a Sorenson sweetie just entered."

Terri often took vocal tallies of the men attending Violet Valley socials, and Jessie had stopped letting it embarrass her long ago. "Isn't your dance card already a little full for tonight?"

Terri shook her head. "I *always* have room on my dance card for a Brewer boy." Her friend practically drooled as she stared at Samuel Brewer, one of Matt's younger brothers who only made an appearance in Violet Valley a few times a year. He loved crowds about as much as Matt did, which made it an eye-popping event to see him at the well-attended Winter Festival.

Several minutes and four customers later, Terri still hadn't taken her eyes off Sam, and Jessie let out a laugh. "If Sam *is* to be the future love of your life, you might want to consider losing the hat."

Terri must have forgotten about the ridiculous thing because she ripped it off her head, fluffing her blonde hair quickly. "Think I should go talk to him?"

"Who are you kidding? You're going to go talk to him whether I think you should or not."

"You're right. How do I look?" She blew the scent of citrus bubblegum at Jessie's face. "Breath okay?"

Jessie laughed again. "Go take a powder and check for yourself."

Terri needed no encouragement, grabbing her purse and knocking her stool into Jessie's leg as she made a beeline for the bathroom.

Johnny Mathis' melodic voice crooned overhead, telling

Jessie to have herself a merry little Christmas as she turned to find Matt heading straight for her with that determined stride. It was then that Fiona Brewer stepped in front of her booth to stare at all the baked goods lining the wall behind Jessie. "Well, goodness," she said, making a tsking sound between her teeth. "You have certainly outdone yourself this time, my dear."

"Hello, Fiona. What a nice surprise," Jessie said without inflection. "How is Tessa's booth doing this year? She's across the hall and I haven't had a chance to make it over for that marmalade."

"Fine," she said, looking distracted. "Just fine."

Jessie braced herself for Fiona's real reason to stop by her booth. She doubted it was to buy baked goods. "What can I get for you, Fiona?"

"Have you seen my son?"

"I'm looking at two of them as we speak," Jessie said, pulling her reserve smile in place for Matt's mother. "In fact, one is standing right behind you."

Fiona turned to see Matt towering over her, his hands clasped behind his back. The older woman jumped back, embarrassed quickly, and then smacked his chest for grinning about it. "Matthew Aaron Brewer! What could you possibly be thinking sneaking up on your mother like that? I'm an old woman. You could have given me a heart attack." She grabbed a limp napkin off the counter and tried fanning her face.

Jessie shared a smile with Matt.

"Sorry, Mother," he muttered, trying to look contrite. "You were looking for me?"

"Yes." The woman quickly realized she'd forgotten what she wanted to say and stood slack-jawed for a moment. "Where is my only grandson? He *is* here, isn't he?"

He grinned. "I believe he's fishing."

She looked appalled. *"What?"*

"Fiona," Jessie said, intervening when it looked like

Matt was having way too much fun teasing his mother. The older woman turned to see Jessie pointing to the fishing booth. They all turned to watch children flooding around the immense blue board with a cartoon fish painted on it. The fish, of course, wore a red Santa hat, as any decent Christmas fish would. Brody poked his nose through the hole that served as the fish's large mouth and made a little boy giggle. After readying the end of his fishing line with a dollar, the child tossed the clothespin through the hole. Brody quickly tied a small trinket to the end of the line and pulled twice. The boy yanked hard on the plastic pole, jerking the toy through the hole and squealing with delight when the toy surprise hit him in the face.

"My goodness," Fiona said, a hand going to her chest, "that is a hideous looking thing. When are they going to stop putting that up year after year?"

"When it stops being the most popular booth," Jessie said.

Fiona dabbed her neck with the napkin and looked up to Matt. "Certainly looks like he's having fun."

"Brody likes that it's for charity," Jessie said.

"His psychologist said Brody looks forward to this all year," Matt said, giving a quick wink to Jessie, an all-okay signal regarding the session.

At the mention of Brody's psychologist, Fiona turned to Jessie, her expression faltering between disapproval and intense dislike. She attempted a shaky smile, no doubt for Matt's benefit. "We'd love to have you and Brody at the ranch for the Christmas gathering. I'm sure my son mentioned it to you."

Jessie held her smile in place. There was no need for Matt to mention the Christmas gathering Fiona Brewer put together at the same time every year for her guests and ranch employees. It wasn't on the same scale as the Winter Festival, but it was never anything less than good downhome fun, as were all the Brewer gatherings. If nothing else, Fiona knew how to throw an amazing party, and each year Violet Valley's own residents would reserve rooms at the ranch to attend. "We wouldn't miss it," she said. "Brody loves spending time there."

"Good. I'll ask Tessa to set two extra places," Fiona said, a pointless jab since Tessa always served dinner buffet-style. "So." Fiona attempted another smile. "Will Brody be going back to school after Christmas? I have several friends who have asked me about it."

Jessie's smile remained intact. "I don't know what you mean."

"Mother," Matt said under his breath.

"All I'm saying is that he should be in school with children his own age," Fiona said, those piercing blue eyes still zeroed on Jessie. "That's all I'm saying. Is that bad? I want him to have friends." She turned to Matt. "That doesn't make me an evil grandmother, does it? Am I horrible? Anyone who has ears can tell the poor child is lonely. Why, he's a nonstop chatterbox morning to night from sitting in that house all day. He's lonely. I'm only concerned about him. Is that so bad?"

The pitiful picture Fiona painted would have bothered Jessie had Brody not been that sweet little chatterbox since he could form sounds. When Fiona turned back to her, Jessie had to wonder if her ex-mother-in-law would continue to look at her with that imperious smirk had Jessie ever mentioned the numerous bully beatings Brody had endured before she'd pulled him out of school. Her son may not have friends his own age, but it wasn't for his lack of trying.

"You do understand Jessie is working today," Matt said, his fingertips touching his mother's elbow before he lowered his voice. "And I specifically asked you *not* to do this."

Jessie looked down, pretending not to hear his whispered words.

"Do what?" Fiona turned to Matt again, loud as ever.

"I didn't say anything demeaning. I simply think this homeschooling thing is very odd. I know no one else who does that."

"Plenty of people homeschool, Fiona," Jessie said, unable to stop herself from commenting. "Why, we have several here in Violet Valley."

The older woman turned to Jessie. "Aren't you terrified you'll stunt his growth or something? He may not turn out…normal. I want him to be normal. That's all I'm saying."

Jessie pulled in a patient breath and pointed to the line behind Fiona. "Can I get you a cup of chili or soup, Fiona? Perhaps a baked good?"

Fiona glanced over her shoulder to the customers crowding behind her. She turned back to Jessie, lips pursed as she then took quick inventory of the baked goods against the wall. "I'll take a dozen gluten free pumpkin bars." She cleared her throat. "Stern might have a gluten allergy." She glanced at Matt, whose critical glare had turned to relief. "We should have a diagnosis after I get your father in to see the doctor. You know how he can be. The man is stubborn as a mule."

Matt looked at Jessie and bit down on his lips to keep from laughing. It was impossible for her not to share his amusement. At one point in their marriage, Fiona's stubbornness was one of the only subjects of which they could agree. They'd always held a united front against his mother's chronic disapprovals, and she was grateful for that.

Fiona scribbled off a check to Dowry's Deli and Jessie handed her a package of pumpkin bars. "Merry Christmas, Fiona. Thank you for the invite. I wouldn't miss it for anything."

The woman nodded and grabbed the bars, turning without another word as she headed toward Samuel Brewer, who stood by the Christmas Ales booth, sampling a small glass.

Jessie's next customer asked for six cups of chili and a full plate of cornbread. As she began cutting cornbread, Matt assumed Terri's spot next to her.

"Sorry about that," he said, handing her six disposable cups for the chili. "I saw her heading this way but someone detained me on the way over."

"I noticed," she said, ladling out the chili. "The fan club came out early. You okay?"

"Yeah," he said. "But I'd be better if you'd give me something to do. I feel useless."

She had no time to argue with him. "Terri handles the money."

"Got it." He looked at the prices on the board behind them and quickly became her other half, moving the customers through quickly and efficiently.

When the line had dispersed, she dropped to the floor and began restocking the shelves under the counter for the next lunch rush, moving bowls and cups in closer reach.

He knelt next to her. "When do you close for the day?" he asked, handing her the bowls and cups to make the task easier. "I wanted to talk, if we could."

"I close when the food runs out."

He glanced at the wall of baked goods and paused. "You're going to be here all night."

"That's the idea." She grinned. "Lots of moola, which means I can pay off this debt I owe your brother that much faster."

He frowned. Looked down. "Luke wouldn't want you working yourself into exhaustion to pay him back."

"I won't." She looked up to see the doubt in his eyes and smiled. "I *promise.*"

"Good, because I'm holding you to it."

She could barely contain her excitement. "Ken would have been so proud. We're doing great."

"You mean *you're* doing great. You did all of this, Jess. At least take a little credit."

She felt her face glow under his praise. "Dowry's Deli

is doing better today than we have in years."

"That's because you've added to the menu. Even Pop said your shop is the new talk of the town." He stared at her now with an expression she didn't recognize as he handed her more napkins. "You love this, don't you? Running the show, I mean."

She giggled. "Well, Terri *does* say I'm a control freak."

He smiled with her. "I'm serious. Are you happy?"

"I am. I mean, it's more work than managing the store and doing the baking. But it's so rewarding, Matt. For the first time since my dad moved us here, I finally feel like I belong. But not because Ken took me under his wing or because I married a Brewer. I feel like they've finally accepted me on *my* terms. Does that make sense?"

"It does. And you're holding up great, by the way," he said. "For someone who didn't get much sleep last night. You don't look the least bit tired."

"I should be exhausted and I probably will be later, but right now I feel like I could fly. Even your mother couldn't make a dent in my good mood today." She let out a laugh because she couldn't help herself. "Everything is perfect. The *business* is doing well. *Brody* is happy. And *you're* home—"

She realized what she'd revealed the second his movements halted and their gazes locked. Unable to reel the words back, she looked down to where his fingers still touched hers over a package of plastic spoons. The Great Hall remained a bustle of noise and chaos, but for several seconds, time below the counter stood still. His gaze dropped to her mouth, and before she could explain her comment, his hand cupped her cheek and he was kissing her. She closed her eyes, her heart rising in her throat as his lips lingered, soft and tender. But then his hand fell away and he was pulling back. She opened her eyes to see him looking as disoriented as she felt.

"Sorry," he said, glancing down for something else to hand her.

"What was that for?" she whispered.

"I don't know." He looked anywhere but her. "I didn't plan it."

"You say that a lot these days."

He grabbed another package of napkins and handed it to her. "It's my reality these days. Little planning and a lot of apologies. Where did Terri bolt off to anyway?"

Grateful for the change in subject, she recalled her friend's expression earlier and giggled. "She's in the bathroom preening. One look at Sam walking through that door and she took off to make herself beautiful for him. What can I say…she's crazy and eager." Jessie grabbed the dorky straw hat Terri had been wearing earlier and shook it for emphasis. "She had a bit of work to do, too. This thing was the first to go."

He pulled it from her grip, placed it on her head, and grinned. "Cute."

Her heart squeezed at the sight of those dimples. "Just stop." She whipped it off her head and straightened her hair with a swipe. "I don't want to scare the customers away."

"Like you could." Grabbing her hand, he placed the hat back on her head and stood, pulling her with him before she could take it off again. They laughed together and turned to see the new line of customers that had formed.

And there, front and center, stood Cole McLeod.

CHAPTER NINE

She pulled her hand from Matt's, her smile disintegrating as she grabbed the hat off her head to drop it on the floor behind her. "Cole. Um, *hi*. Here for lunch?"

He smiled at her. "A break, actually." He looked at Matt. Back to her. "I stopped by to drop off the toys for Brody's booth. From the donations."

She glanced at Matt, her cheeks flushing before turning back to Cole. "Thanks," she said, fixing her static-filled hair with another swipe. "That should keep him busy most of the day."

Cole looked to Matt again and an awkward silence settled over the booth.

"Nice to see you again, Cole." Matt nodded, surprised that he'd managed to say the words without using what Jessie had termed as a *SARS* or *smallpox* tone. It had taken great effort, too. He didn't have anything personal against Cole McLeod. Had considered him a friend until recently. Now if he could just keep the guy at least a hundred yards away from Jessie at all times, he'd feel even better about the situation.

Jessie looked up at Matt, another appreciative smile for his effort.

"You too, Matt." Cole returned the nod before turning back to Jessie. "Thought I'd get a cup of your great coffee while I'm here. To go."

"O-oh." She practically stuttered, suddenly clumsy as a three-legged giraffe as she reached for a stack of cups and knocked it off the counter. "S-sure thing." She looked to the group standing behind him, every one of them watching the moment unfold with interest.

Jessie's eyebrows furrowed and Matt finally understood her nervousness. It wasn't Cole. It was the gossip. She didn't want to be the center of it, and a love triangle in Violet Valley—real or fiction—was fodder for a torrent of whispers that would keep lips moving until June.

He looked past Cole to watch Terri leave Sam's side and head back toward Dowry's booth. Perfect timing for him to talk to his brother about the new company. He turned to find Jessie fumbling with a cup under the coffee dispenser and he reached over, placing a hand gently over her wrist.

She looked up, startled by the intimate gesture in front of Cole and God and the whole of Violet Valley.

"I have to go talk to Sam," he said, low so only she could hear. "Terri's headed this way. You okay here for a while?"

She nodded, shoulders sagging slightly. "Thanks for your help, Matt." Her hands trembled badly as she released coffee into the cup. "Would you mind grabbing lunch for Brody at another booth and taking it over to him? Kelley isn't due for another hour, if she shows up at all, and he must be starving already. He'd probably love someone else's cooking for a change."

He frowned, watching her shaking hands and remembering the illness she now struggled to control. PTSD was nothing to mess with. "No problem."

"Thanks." She gave him another appreciative smile. "You have no idea. My lifesaver. Big time."

He pressed his fingers to the small of her back, a

lasting, intimate gesture to let her and everyone else—*Cole*—know that he wouldn't be far away.

He turned in time to intercept Terri, who crashed into his chest and dropped her purse, along with a handful of paper bowls. "Oh my goodness—it's like hitting a wall," she muttered, bending to pick up her things. He helped her straighten while attempting to step around her. She glowered at him. "Hey, where do you think you're going? You can't go."

He hadn't heard from Terri since receiving her voicemail over a month ago—something neither had yet acknowledged to the other—and once again, she sounded mad as a hornet. He shrugged. "Looks like you two have it under control."

"Are you blind? This is a mob. We'll never catch up. You *have* to stay. Tell him Jessie." Terri looked at Jessie's back before her attention snapped to Cole, her eyes narrowing. "Um…Cole?" she said, grabbing McLeod's attention from Jessie. "What are you doing here?"

"Getting a coffee." He returned her scowl with a smug, taunting expression that reminded Matt of grade school, making him wonder how many more run-ins these two had already had over Jessie. "Why? Is that a crime?"

"No," she said, "but you should get back to your patrol car. I saw someone letting air out of the tires."

McLeod stared at her, clearly unconvinced.

"Don't believe me?" Terri asked while Jessie turned and handed McLeod his coffee. "Come on. I'll be happy to show you."

Terri was anything but subtle, and Matt had difficulty not smiling, thankful she appeared to be on his side when it came to Cole McLeod. Matt made his way to the Fish-n-Chips booth, paid for a sweet tea and a paper bowl of the deep fried food, and headed for the Christmas fishing booth next to it. The place was still in full swing—kids everywhere—as he made his way behind the oversized fish and sat next to Brody on the concrete floor, appreciating the solitude from the crowded hall. The kid had the best seat in town. His boy finished hooking a toy to a clothespin, pulled twice, and glanced over at Matt. "Hey, Dad. Pretty sweet turnout, huh?"

"Pretty sweet, indeed," he agreed, leaning against the wall as he watched Brody work. "Your booth is more popular than your mom's. She sent me over with provisions, by the way. Fish and chips."

"Oh man." His eyes rounded. "I'm starved. Thanks."

"When do you close the booth?"

Brody grinned. "When I run out of presents. Cole just brought me two more bags of toys." He nodded to the two black bags against the wall. "Mom's store donated the money this year, although I'm not supposed to tell anyone. But she didn't have time to get the toys last night with all the prep work and asked Cole to do it."

His stomach churned acid to think of her phoning Cole McLeod for anything, much less for help. He pulled his hat off and ran a hand through his hair, trying to control the jealousy coursing through him. Even remembering the simple handshake he'd witnessed that first night made him want to break McLeod's arm. "You like Cole a great deal, don't you?"

Brody took a bite of the fish, chewing. "He's nice. He said if I want to be a cop when I get older, that he'd give me a…a leg up." A clothespin flew through the hole and hit Brody in the back of the head. His face bloomed crimson and he turned, looking out the hole and sticking out his tongue, which only caused the child on the other side to laugh.

Matt pulled on his hat firmly. "Wow, I didn't realize this was such a dangerous job."

His son smirked, pulling the dollar from the clothespin and stuffing it into a large coffee tin. "It's not. But you have to pay attention." He dug through the still half-full bag and found a toy, latching it with the clothespin and pulling twice.

The toy yanked through the hole and Brody crammed five steak fries into his mouth. "He also listens to me when I talk," he murmured with his mouth full.

"Cole?"

"Yeah. Most grownups don't."

"You don't think I listen to you?"

Brody shrugged. "You do when you're here. But you're never here."

The kid had said the statement without judgment but with such certainty that Matt paused. He'd been away on assignment what amounted to six months, likely much more, of each year of his child's life, and he'd missed his son tremendously during that time. But he'd tried not to dwell on his absence from his son's life too much, probably because he'd always felt he was in the way whenever he returned home from an assignment, as if he were messing up Jessie's process. But now he knew the truth. Everyone had noticed his absence profoundly, most of all Jessie and Brody. How could he ever make up for so much lost time?

"Are you and Mom getting back together?" Brody asked, dodging the next clothespin that flew through the hole.

"I couldn't tell you, buddy." He glanced at his son, who sucked tea noisily through a straw in one long drink. "That seems to be the question."

"You don't know?" he asked, still chewing.

"Not at the moment."

Brody latched a clothespin to another toy, this time tossing it back through the hole instead of yanking the string. "Are you going to die, Dad?"

Matt's heart missed a beat. "Not any time soon, I hope. Why would you ask me that?"

Brody frowned. "Aunt Terri comes over often when you're gone. I've heard them talking in the kitchen when they thought I was asleep." Another bite of fish. "And it sounds like you're gonna die. Mom cried. She cries a lot.

So I was wondering if you're gonna die."

He couldn't have felt like a bigger deadbeat if the kid had called him one. "I'm not going to die, Brody."

"Really?"

"Yeah."

"Good."

"How long have you worried like this?"

"A long time." He pushed four more fries into his mouth before busying himself with another clothespin. "So you should get married again," he murmured almost unintelligibly with a full mouth. "I like it better when you're home. Mom doesn't cry as much. She just yells more."

If the statement hadn't gutted him to hear, he might have laughed at Brody's matter-of-fact tone. "You know what would be cool?"

Brody snorted to hear his dad say the word *cool*. "What?"

"What if your mom could be happy for once? No crying or yelling. How would that be?"

Brody's eyebrow arched and he swallowed some of the food. "Would you be there?"

"I plan to be."

He yanked on the string. "Yeah, that'd be cool." Then glanced at Matt. "I like that better."

"Which means I have a lot to figure out and I'd better get to it," he said, pushing himself off the cement floor. "I'm going to go talk to your Uncle Sam, but I'll be around here somewhere if you need me."

"Uncle Sam's here?"

"Yep. We both could use a new line of work and I asked him to stop by to discuss a business venture together."

"Like a company?"

"Yep."

"Awesome." Brody grinned just before a clothespin hit him in the ear. "Gah! Quit throwing so hard!" he yelled through the hole while rubbing his ear red.

Squeals of laughter rang out in response.

"I'd better go. This is dangerous business," Matt said, pointing to him. "Remember to watch your eyes."

"What?"

"Be careful of those clothespins when looking through the porthole."

"It's not a porthole, Dad; it's a fish mouth." Brody rolled his eyes. "I'm the Christmas fish, remember?"

Matt grinned. His son, the Christmas fish. He wouldn't have had it any other way.

*****

Most of the booths had closed, the first band had started, and the dancing had commenced before Jessie finally called it quits and asked Matt to take an exhausted Brody home and put him to bed. In a blatant effort to get Jessie to go with them, Terri coerced Sam into helping her and Kelley tear down the booth. Jessie took that opportunity to drive the few remaining baked items—as well as a beautiful blue ribbon for Most Deliciously Inventive—back to the deli.

It was late when she finally arrived home, and as excited as she was about the prospect of sleep, the notion of getting out of the car and into bed was a daunting one. Her feet ached and every muscle hurt, but she grabbed her purse and three jars of Tessa's marmalade and opened the car door. She sighed, needing a push. If only someone would carry her up the porch stairs now and put *her* to bed, she could call this day a complete success.

She heard Matt talking on his phone in the kitchen when she opened the front door. The remainder of the house was silent and dark, proof that Brody had likely passed out in bed as soon as they got home—the usual ending to his participation in one of Violet Valley's social affairs.

The teapot began to whistle like an alarm announcing her arrival, and she found Matt cutting off his call as he pulled the kettle off the stove.

He didn't turn as she placed her purse and the three jam jars on the counter. No surprise. A man in his profession had to be aware of everything. He likely knew the exact sound of her car.

"I figured you'd be crashed on the couch," she said, removing her coat and throwing it over a dining chair to rub her eyes. "Not making us tea."

He looked at her. "Why's that?"

She arched her eyebrows as he pulled two cups off their hooks. "Because crowds bother you."

"*Bothered* me," he corrected with a grin, those dimples poking through his five o'clock shadow as he poured hot water over two tea bags. "I'm a new man, remember? Or at least trying to be."

"You can't just turn off something like that, Matt."

"No, you're right." He placed the kettle on the back of the stove. "But I'm not going to work through the issue by continuing to avoid it. The problem started when I first went away. I just need to find my way back. And I intend to."

She didn't know how to respond to that. He was acting so differently. But the same. Comfortably familiar, and sexy and exciting and different and…

She needed sleep in the worst way.

"And as predicted, *you* look beat," he said, crossing the kitchen and handing her one of the hot cups.

"I am." She smiled as she took it. "I think I have a headache coming on, too."

"That's because you carry all of your stress in your shoulders. I'd offer you a neck rub but you'd probably be asleep inside of a minute. And it's important tonight that I keep you awake. I was hoping we could still have that talk before I leave."

She blew at her tea and turned for the living room, pretending that disappointment didn't gnaw at her. He'd be leaving tonight, back to the ranch, and she didn't want him to go. Things had been different between them lately. She'd forgotten it could be like this. In truth, she wanted him to stay, and she still wasn't sure how she felt about that. "Well, I'm not making any promises. I'll try to stay up a while longer though. I don't have work tomorrow, which is good since I may not be able to get off this sofa once I sit down. But if I start snoring, please don't take it personally. Just throw a blanket over me and let yourself out."

His brief laugh had a nervous edge as he followed her to the couch. "This idea I'm about to spring on you is pretty radical. I'm hoping you can keep an open mind."

She sat and steeled herself with a sip of the green tea, grateful for the heat that burned the remaining chill from her bones. She placed her cup on the end table and pulled a blue couch pillow between them like an emotional shield, their knees nearly touching then when he turned to face her. "I'm not going to like this, am I?" she asked.

"Probably not."

She wasn't up for bad news, but his worried expression made her ask anyway. "What is it?"

He took a swallow of his tea and set it on the coffee table, rubbing a hand through his short hair before sliding forward and bracing his elbows on his knees. "Sam and I are starting a business."

She stared at him, a half-smile screwing onto her face as she waited for the punch line.

"A small PI group," he explained when she didn't say anything, "and it's really more Sam's thing. A venture he's been talking about for a couple of years. He's wanted to get out of police life for a while and this is a natural progression for him, forward or backward, depending how you look at it. But it seems to be what he wants to do. I think he needs this." He let out a shaky breath, the first indication that he wasn't joking. Her ex-husband was made of steel. *Nervous* wasn't in his DNA. Why then did he just wipe his palms on his jeans? "When I decided to retire a few months ago, I figured Sam might find my specific skillset useful, so I asked him if he wanted to make it a joint undertaking. We've been talking about it off and on ever since. Two days ago, I called him to make it official."

Her eyes widened. "That's why he stopped by today? Because you called him?"

He nodded. "We wanted to work out a few of the details, which we did. At length. That's why I disappeared this afternoon, if you were wondering."

She looked down at the coffee table, waiting for the hazy, surreal feeling to dissipate and the news to sink in. It all felt loose, and fuzzy and wonderful, like slowly waking from a dream.

"We'd have to base the company in Atlanta," he continued. "It's the only location close to Violet Valley that makes sense. We couldn't pull off a business like that in a smaller town. It'll also be a massive pay cut, at least for me. And the commute is terrible."

She lifted her gaze to his, not at all sure what to say. The wonderful ache forming in her chest was overwhelming—what she imagined was the beginning of certain happiness that could be hers if he wasn't joking. "I guess I'm still waiting for the bad news. Because this doesn't sound like bad news, Matt."

"Well, there's more. But my point is, much of the work I'll be doing I can do by phone and laptop, which would free me up to be *here*, in Violet Valley, most of the time for Brody. To help him with school or his work at the ranch or…anything else." He swallowed hard, his dark gaze fixed on the coffee table. "And to be here for you. If you need me."

That wonderful ache quickly transformed into a lump of raw emotion that rose and lodged in her throat. She swallowed, close to tears. "Y-you're really leaving that life behind?"

He still wouldn't look at her. "Yes."

Her eyes watered until she could no longer see. She

blinked rapidly, having wanted this so badly for so long that she was terrified to believe him. To hope. "Is that what you want?"

His gaze slid to hers, as determined as she'd ever seen him. "I have no doubts, Jess. When I retire, I'm never going back. I swear it."

He meant it. She could read it in his eyes. Truth. Sincerity. And for once, she believed him.

"Please say something," he said.

She looked down, fighting the tide of tears and gratitude for all her unanswered prayers. Unanswered until now. She tried to think of anything that would stop her trembling chin and quivering lip from coaxing up the torrent of bottled emotion simmering just beneath the surface. She pushed a hand over her mouth. Tried pulling in a breath. And then that dense ache in her throat tightened until it finally broke free in the most pitiful sob that she'd ever heard. One she couldn't control. Everything blurred through tears and she pushed her face into her hands, mortified to be ruining the moment, the *news,* she'd waited a decade to hear. "I'm sorry," she cried, "I don't mean to—"

She felt his arms surround her before she could utter another word. She didn't bother to suggest she was okay. Her limbs shook terribly as she put her arms around him. She'd never broken down like this in front of anyone, and it embarrassed her enough to hide her face in the crook of his neck. He was here. Permanently. Finally. Safe in her arms. Home to stay. She wrapped herself tightly against him when hugging couldn't possibly get her close enough.

"I'm so sorry for doing this to you," he said against her hair. "If I'd had any idea what this was doing to you all of this time—*nothing* is worth that to me. You have to believe me. Can you ever forgive me?"

"Shhh," she whispered against his neck, and then giggled to realize she was the one shushing him. She pulled back to look at him, unable to remember a happier moment. "Just kiss me."

His face was a blur through her tears, his expression uncertain as he hesitated briefly before lowering his head to hers. The second their lips touched, she sighed, moaning then when he quickly deepened the kiss and threaded his fingers through her hair to pull her closer. Her tongue brushed against his, drinking him in as she wove her fingers inside his navy cotton shirt, releasing a button with her thumb, then another, until the material opened to expose the stretched black t-shirt underneath. She smoothed her hand against his abdomen, feeling the muscles tighten under her touch as she pulled the shirt from his jeans, desperate to feel his skin. To be as close as they could be.

"Jess," he whispered, what sounded like a question, but his lips quickly found hers again, dousing any notion she had of him stopping her. She didn't want to stop. She wanted this. Under his skin. Feeling him breathe.

She pushed forward, in his arms one moment, his lap the next, and then she was straddling his hips as he pulled her flush against him. They moved slowly with each kiss, soon mimicking making love, and she desperately wanted to, unable to get close enough soon enough.

He lowered his head to her neck, whispered something against her skin, his lips hot and wet and blazing a trail back to her mouth. She could no longer tell who was leading what. His hands glided under her sweater and up her sides, causing a trail of goosebumps to follow. When her sweater became too much of an impediment, she gripped the hem to remove it.

Suddenly and without warning, his hands were at her elbows, stopping her. *"Wait."*

The movement jerked her forward slightly and she caught herself against his chest, only a fraction from another kiss. It would have been that easy. But the jolt had caused her dreamlike state to dissipate and she lifted her gaze from that perfectly shaped mouth to those blue eyes, her breaths rushing in and out along with his as she waited for an explanation.

"Sorry, I didn't mean that," he said, brushing her hair back and framing her face before kissing her softly.

"You didn't mean what?"

"To startle you like that." He dropped back against the couch. "Or for that kiss to go that far." His chest moved up and down, matching the quick rhythm of his heart that pounded hard under her fingertips, same as hers. Uncertainty battled the fire in his eyes as he brushed the back of his hand against her jaw. His body felt tense and coiled underneath her, his desire still obvious. So why was he stopping what they both wanted?

"Please don't ruin this," she whispered.

"You have no idea how much I want you right now," he said. "But there's more. I haven't told you everything. And this can't be right between us until I tell you everything."

She searched his eyes, her heart sinking. The bad news. She'd been too caught up in the moment to notice the warning bells. In the past, he wouldn't have bothered to stop her and she wouldn't have thought twice about rushing in. In the past, they had taken every stolen moment of happiness they could get, which made his warning—this gesture of trust—so much more endearing and important. But no matter how right or logical it would be for her to listen, she couldn't hear his news. Not now. "Not yet," she whispered.

"It's important, Jess. You need to know."

She brushed the tip of her finger over his lips. "What I need is to be happy," she said softly. "And you've made me happy tonight. *So* happy, Matt. Let me have this. You and me. *Us.* No complications. Just for a while." She leaned in and kissed him, soft and brief. "Later. You can tell me later. *After.*"

His fingers brushed her hair back as she lingered close to his mouth. "Even if what I tell you changes everything?"

"Nothing will change how I feel right now," she whispered.

He studied her expression, her certainty, pausing only seconds before meeting her halfway, his remaining resistance cracking the second her lips touched his. He gripped her thighs, his kiss demanding and stealing her breath as he shifted forward and stood, lifting her with him and walking to the bedroom where there would be no interruptions.

For the briefest moment, her mind tried to overrule, to make her stop what could later lead to terrible heartache. But then he shut the door behind them, he lowered her onto the bed, and she knew she was exactly where she wanted to be.

She pushed the material from his shoulders, peeling away the navy button-down and throwing it onto the floor. His black t-shirt followed, revealing those hard muscles to her touch. He moved quickly, removing her sweater, her bra, and scooping her in his embrace as his mouth moved hot down her neck, trailing a path to her breast where she arched against each incredible sensation. Everything he did felt slow and deliberate, as if he planned to take his time. To torture her endlessly until she cried out his name. He might have too, but she couldn't wait. "I need you," she whispered. "Now."

It was always the same when they'd been apart too long, and their next hurried movements left a wake of their remaining clothes on the floor, blankets pushed back, and then his skin was against hers, he was sliding inside her, and they were no longer apart. She pulled in a breath, taking him all in, whole and complete as he held her tightly. She closed her eyes, gliding her fingertips down his back, wishing that the moment could draw out forever.

But perfection couldn't last, and when he kissed her again with a need that matched her own, desire took over and she held on tightly, keeping her thighs wrapped against his hips as they found their rhythm again, slow at first, until they were moving together with swift strokes, until she could no longer hold back. She arched and climaxed quickly as wave after wave washed over her. And then his mouth covered hers, his kiss heated and demanding as he quickly found his release with her.

*****

She'd needed a glass of water. That's what she'd told him when she left for the master bath to splash cold water on her face. Now she couldn't stop staring at her reflection in the mirror, wondering where this person had been for the last two years. She looked like a stranger. Flushed. Eyes shining. And what was with that whimsical smile that kept pulling at the corners of her mouth? She looked...happy.

She remembered being happy for a long time. And then she wasn't. It was like a cycle with them. And now she had to prepare herself for the unhappy. The bad news.

It was time to pay the piper.

She turned and opened the door quietly. Matt was on his back, his forearm thrown behind his head as he stared at the ceiling. His eyes looked dark, his expression grim before he turned to watch her padding quietly across the carpet toward the bed.

He rolled onto his side and up on his elbow as she slid under the covers next to him, resting her cheek on her pillow.

He studied her a long moment. "I have to ask you something."

"What?" She brushed the soft sheet between them to avoid his intense gaze.

He reached out and looped a long, dark tendril behind her ear, only to watch it fall forward again. "Are you still on the pill?"

She glanced at him, unable to stop a shy smile. He looked a little nervous and genuinely interested to hear the answer. Asking after the fact, though, was a little late for concern. Not that it mattered. She'd been on the pill when they'd conceived Brody. She hadn't had much faith in contraception after that, although she'd still used it faithfully until the divorce. "Your romantic side knows no bounds, Matt. No, really. You might want to turn down the charm a little before I start to blush."

"You're already blushing." He returned her smile before asking again, "So are you?"

"On the pill?" She dropped her gaze to his chest, then to the trail of dark hair that disappeared underneath the blankets. She finally worked up the nerve to look at him again, her voice barely above a whisper. "No."

That curious, gentle expression crossed his features again. He pulled his own pillow closer to hers and rested his head against it, a mirror image of her position. His fingertips drifted over her hip, then her waist. "God, I'd love it if you got pregnant tonight," he said.

"Matt," she whispered, pulling the blankets closer to her chest, a small barrier to separate them as her cheeks heated. "Don't say that."

He slowly pulled his hand from her waist, his eyes searching hers. "Where do you see this leading, Jess? Because a few minutes ago you looked happy to be with me. And now...I can't figure out that expression. Regret?"

"No. It's not that. I told you I wanted us to have this." She reached out to him, pressing her fingers softly against the top of his hand. The uneasiness in his eyes likely mirrored hers. She didn't want to hurt him. That wasn't her intention. But as the one between them who still didn't have all the facts, she doubted she could be of any comfort to either of them.

"Then what is it?"

"I guess I'm trying to prepare for the bad news. That's all."

He looked down and swallowed hard, his reluctance stretching her nerves tight. Past-Matt didn't hesitate like this. He didn't second-guess himself. So when his gaze finally rested on hers again, her heart pounded in preparation. "A year ago I accepted a job," he said. "One I can't get out of."

She pressed her lips together, thinking about what he'd said. "When do you leave?" The softly spoken question was an automatic response after years of receiving the same news. He often accepted assignments months before execution. There were preparations to make. People to hire. Debriefings to hold. Precautions to take. Possibly vaccinations, depending where they were sending him.

"Two days after Christmas."

She nodded. "Okay." Her voice sounded oddly normal and accepting for someone not fully connected to the moment. But then her mouth turned down, her chin quivered, and she blinked rapidly—her body's tearful response to news her mind still hadn't fully registered.

"Jessie." He reached over and stroked her cheek.

His tender touch was her undoing, and tears dribbled over her lashes. "You said no more, Matt." More tears followed. "You said you were done."

"I am done. I swear it." The pad of his thumb brushed back several tears. "*After* this. I accepted this job over a year ago. Certain things have already been set into motion. I can't get out of it. You know how this works, Jess."

"You're right. I do. I also know you could get someone else if you wanted to." She curled into herself, closing her eyes to try to separate herself from him and this life that continued to repeat itself. But she couldn't do it. Old fears quickly rushed in, and a sob slipped from her throat as denial slipped from her grasp. She curled into herself tighter. "You swore, Matt. You promised."

"I promised you I was retiring and I am."

Semantics. Always semantics with Matt. He'd told her everything she'd wanted to hear. And she'd heard exactly what she'd wanted to hear. He hadn't lied. He just hadn't told her the full truth.

"They can't get someone else." He brushed her hair back, making her look at him. "Listen, this isn't my ego talking. I swear it. I can't get out of it because I accepted a retainer months ago. I'm bought and paid for, Jess. My entire crew. The client needed me to be available at a specific time and that's how it's done, Jess. It's too late. There's nothing I can do."

She closed her eyes tightly. "Give it back." Desperation forced the words out, making her sound like a child in an anxiety-filled tantrum. She didn't care. "We don't need the money. Just…give the retainer back and get someone else to do it."

"I can't," he said.

"Why?" She opened her eyes, lifting her gaze to his. "Give me one good reason."

"Because there's nothing left to give back."

Stunned, her tears stopped abruptly. "What do you mean there's nothing left?"

"I mean it's gone. All of it. Spent."

"Spent?" A sudden flash of anger coursed through her and she pushed him back. Wiped her eyes. Pulled the blankets to her chest and sat upright to face him. "I am *not* stupid, Matt. You're saying this as an excuse to leave again. I naively thought things had changed and now we're right back to square one."

"I swear to you, I'm not lying about this—"

"I don't believe you," she said, interrupting him. "*You* don't buy things, Matt. Ever. You're the most frugal person in the world. You find zero joy in money. We wouldn't even have this house had I not asked for it. All you do is earn and save. Work, work, work. Save, save, save. It's what you do. It's the theme of our entire marriage, for petesake. There's *no* way you would have spent that kind of money." She looked down at him. "Now quit treating me like someone who doesn't know you. Tell me the truth."

"I told you the truth." He pulled himself upright, facing her as the blankets dropped to his waist. "But it's complicated."

"Of course it is." She scrubbed her face, so very tired. "Everything is always so complicated with you."

"I wired it to Luke."

Her gaze swung to him. *"What?"*

"I gave it to Luke."

"Luke? What would Luke ever need with—" The question disintegrated as the slow realization of what had happened all those months ago occurred to her, and just that quickly, her confusion surrounding Luke's sudden offer to loan her the money was gone. Her questions answered. Luke worked a ranch, and even without rent, he had extensive medical and physical therapy bills from the car accident that would likely follow him throughout his life. He never would have had that much money to give her. But she'd been desperate and hadn't questioned it. Not aloud. Not to him.

She swallowed and looked down at the comforter, trying to get her bearings as her reality once again took a sideways turn. Matt had kept this secret from her all of this time. For months. Her lips trembled, turned down, and she pushed a shaky hand over her mouth.

"Don't blame him, Jess," he said, his voice firm. "He never wanted to lie to you. That was me. It was all me. Blame me."

Fresh tears fell over her lashes. "I *do* blame you," she whispered, turning then and curling against him as she wrapped her arms around his neck. He hesitated only seconds before pulling her into his arms. "We were in the middle of a divorce." She sniffled and shook her head, tears streaming as she buried her face into his neck. "Who does that for someone in the middle of a divorce?"

He brushed her hair back and kissed her temple. "Ken had just passed away," he said softly. "I knew what he meant to you. He was a mentor. A father figure. More than your real dad. And we were no longer together. I couldn't be there for you. But I could do this. I could do *something.*"

She pressed her palm to his rough cheek, pulling his

mouth to hers as she kissed him through her tears, certain that she'd never loved him more. "Stay with me?"

He shifted their bodies, pressing her back against the sheets and pulling the blankets over them as he covered her body with his. This time when he made love to her, he took his time, reminding her just how well he knew her body, her heart, and it wasn't until the early morning hours when she finally drifted to sleep, curled in his arms, exhausted and wishing that he wouldn't have to leave. She'd spent her lifetime wishing and hoping for a permanent life with him, and she was oh so close to having what she wanted. But one final assignment would be tempting fate, and the dread that came with that knowledge followed her into her dreams.

CHAPTER TEN

"Mom!"

A loud knock sounded and Matt opened his eyes, staring at the ceiling as the details of last night rushed in. He remembered locking the bedroom door, which kept him from bolting upright to find his clothes. Instead, he stayed right where he was, enjoying the warmth of her body still tangled with his as a deep satisfaction ran through him. He never wanted to leave her side again.

"Mom!" Another knock.

She stirred, her head shifting across his chest until that silky hair fell over her eyes. "Whaaat?" she murmured against his skin, half-asleep.

"Dad's SUV is still here."

"Great," she whispered, shifting again until she'd propped her chin on his chest to look at him. "I didn't think this through when I invited you to stay."

"Is Dad still here?"

Matt silently laughed as she stirred onto her elbows and said over her shoulder, "Your dad accidentally fell asleep here last night, sweetie. He's in the shower."

Silence.

"Really?" Brody asked. "I don't hear the water

running."

Matt laughed again and she smacked his chest. "Laugh it up, bub," she whispered, her cheeks turning pink. "This is awkward. What should I say?"

"I'm heading to the shower now, kiddo," Matt said, the sleepiness still in his voice.

Silence.

She smacked Matt's chest again and he grinned at her.

"Okay," Brody finally said. "I'm making us breakfast."

"Why did you say that?" she whispered, swiping her hair back before snuggling into his arms. "Now he probably thinks you slept in here with me."

"We've shared the same bedroom all of his life, Jess. Besides, I doubt we can hide this. Not when I intend to stay by your side until I go," he said, tightening his arm around her and pulling her closer. "And right this moment, I want to stay in this bed with you a while longer. You feel too good to leave."

She brushed her lips against his chest and soon he felt wetness on his arm that could only be more tears.

Guilt nagged at him and he sighed, whispering, "Are you going to be okay, Jess? When I go?"

She nodded, but he feared she was just telling him what he wanted to hear, which only made him worry more.

"How long is the assignment?" she whispered.

The dreaded question. "Three months."

She paused. "And the blackout period?"

"Same."

She nodded again, resting her cheek against his chest. "This must be one of the bad ones," she murmured. "A blackout for the length of the assignment?" She stayed silent another minute. "Is it high risk?"

Only in his worst nightmare would he tell her the details of a job. The risks in any of his assignments were high. Whenever she asked, which she didn't very often, he was thankful his contract ordered him to keep his mouth shut. She knew he couldn't answer her.

"Is it?" she asked.

"Jess," he whispered, kissing her forehead and hugging her tightly against his side. "Don't. Okay?"

"Sorry."

She brushed her hand over his abdomen repeatedly, drifting off into her imagination that was likely conjuring up gruesome images. Time to change the topic. "I was meaning to ask you last night," he said. "Why haven't you put up a Christmas tree?"

She placed her hand on his chest and rested her chin there. Looked at him with those shining eyes. "There hasn't been time this year. I was hoping to do that today. Why do you think Brody is up so early? I told him a week ago we'd pick a tree after the festival."

He smiled. "Good. Then I can make myself useful by doing a few manly things around the house today."

"What manly things?"

"Tree pickup. Tree setup. *Macho* things."

"You're incorrigible." She laughed softly. "But Brody will be thankful. He tried doing it himself last year but didn't secure the tree tightly enough. It fell over, lights, ornaments and all."

He grinned. "I wish I'd seen that one."

"No you don't," she said. "He was mad. I mean *really* mad. Meltdown mad."

"Math mad?"

She laughed at his reference. "Exactly. His ears turned red. You know he's mad when those ears turn red. Speaking of meltdowns, we have to decide how we'll explain this to him. You leaving again, I mean. He thinks you're staying. He's not going to understand *one last job,* Matt. I barely understand it."

"I'll tell him," he said. "I created this mess."

"We'll do it," she said. "Remember? Together?"

"Hey, you guys," Brody said through the door. "Do you want pancakes?"

Matt smiled at her. "Pancakes are good, buddy," he

said. Jessie kissed his shoulder and shifted to get out of bed. He reluctantly pulled away to sit upright, glancing at her pretty profile as she tried to fix her rumpled hair with several swipes of her hand. He'd missed this with her. Ordinary life. Pancakes with their son on a Sunday morning. It was all he wanted. "Has he made pancakes before?"

"Not that I'm aware," she said, grabbing her bathrobe from the end of the bed. "I'd better get out there before he burns down my kitchen."

He stared at her back, frowning at her ribs and spine that showed prominently before she pulled her bathrobe around her. He'd never seen her more fragile, physically and emotionally, and he felt responsible.

She turned to him and he quickly covered his concern with a smile before she leaned over the bed and kissed him. He watched her go, his heart heavier than he could remember. She'd taken the news better than he'd expected. She'd never been violent before, but he wouldn't have been surprised last night had she'd slapped him across the face. He'd expected her to accuse him of trying to take over by setting up the loan. For interfering and not trusting her to take care of herself. What he hadn't expected were tears of gratitude, and ultimately, acceptance.

His son, on the other hand, might not take the news as well, and he didn't want to ruin his boy's Christmas. He'd wait until after the holiday. Right before leaving. It would probably take him that long to figure out how to sum up a complicated situation in a way that his overanalyzing son would understand.

*****

They'd spent a perfect family day together, decorating a tree that Brody had picked out at the tree lot. Jessie, still exhausted from the festival, parked herself on the sofa and graded one of Brody's essays as Matt cooked dinner—a roasted chicken and new potatoes recipe that didn't turn out half bad, if he did say so himself.

They spent the next week much as Matt imagined their life would be like when he returned from his last assignment. He divided his attention between Brody, his schoolwork, the ranch, and a growing list of details with his brother, Sam, who was eager to get going on the new business. He also received a call from Max to confirm his arrival in DC after Christmas—the final meeting before his assignment would begin.

Jessie grew quieter with each passing day, throwing herself into her work as she always did when she worried. She managed to get away from the deli twice to join them at the ranch for Brody's hippotherapy training. In the evenings, they took time together as a family, and during the nights, Jessie gave herself to Matt without reservation. Ten years of conflict seemed to melt away, reminding him how happy they'd been before he'd made a decision that had ultimately destroyed their marriage.

But putting the past behind them proved to be easier said than done. Jessie's nightly rituals had changed during their time apart, and it surprised him how often she woke throughout the night, sometimes crying in her sleep, other times bolting upright out of a dream. Each time he'd ask, and each time she avoided the question with a trip to the bathroom. By the fourth night, the I-need-a-glass-of-water routine had worn him thin and he stopped asking. Not surprising, her trips to the bathroom ceased as well. But her nightmares didn't. Desperate, he began pulling her against him in a pre-emptive move the second she started to moan and stir. He'd hold her like that until she settled into a quiet sleep again—a routine that quickly became a habit he did half-asleep.

The days turned into a week, and through all of it, she never once brought up her expectations. Where did she want this to go? She hadn't mentioned love. Did she want to remarry? Stay divorced? Ride this out until the next disagreement? Was this a new beginning for them? Or a kind ending because he'd helped her business during the divorce?

With the assignment looming, he didn't think he could handle any answer that wasn't a lifetime commitment, so he never asked.

The Double-B Christmas bash had a great turnout, and seeing his entire family was worth putting up with his mother's constant henpecking. Besides, with the whole Brewer clan in one place, Fiona Brewer had to choose her browbeating battles. Seeing everyone with Jess and Brody by his side, especially on the cusp of another assignment that he now dreaded, had been exactly what Matt needed to get him into a holiday frame of mine.

Spending Christmas Day with Jessie and Brody soothed his heart in ways he couldn't have imagined. They were happy again, a family, and he wanted to hold onto it.

But life always had a way of intervening.

When it came time to tell Brody, Jessie insisted she be there to help ease the blow, and Matt was thankful for the backup when Brody collapsed onto the bed in tears.

"You're a liar!" Brody gripped the slats of his headboard and closed his eyes. "You said you were staying and now you're leaving. You're a liar. A liar! I hate you!"

"Brody—" Jess whispered, but Matt stepped forward.

"I didn't lie to you," he said. "I'm retiring. Even my employer knows. This is it for me. The last trip. I promise."

"You've said that before." Brody's teary gaze pivoted to his mom. "And you'll let him go. Like you always do. If you do, then I *hate* you, too!"

Matt clenched his teeth to hear his son talk to Jessie like that. "Brody—"

"It's not up to me, honey," she said softly.

Matt mulled over what he could do and sat next to his son, putting a hand on his back. He'd expected the kid to push his arm away but he didn't, which meant there was room for understanding. "I promised someone long ago

I'd do this. I have to keep my promise. Can you understand that?"

"What about your promises to *me?* To *Mom?*" His tear-filled gaze turned to Matt, accusations burning behind those blue eyes.

As much as he wanted to explain, the truth was complicated and more than Brody could understand. Too much detail caused too much confusion. "It's more complicated than that, Brody. I can't really explain why."

"You're gonna die, Dad." Brody pulled away from Matt's hand. "You carry a gun when you go, and guns kill people."

Surprised by the comment, Matt looked to Jessie, who shrugged helplessly. "The school prepared the kids for an active shooter lockdown a few months ago," she said softly. "It was one of the last assemblies he attended before we started homeschooling. He was pretty shaken afterward."

Frowning, he turned and put a hand on Brody's shoulder. "Hey. Come on, kiddo. I'm not a novice. I was in the military. Remember? I train people to do this all the time. I know what I'm doing."

"Lots of people think they know what they're doing. And then they die. And you'll be one of them. Then we'll be alone again, Mom and me. And she'll cry. Because you make her cry, Dad. Every time you go." Brody pulled his head back an inch then and hit his forehead hard against the headboard.

Startled, Matt reacted quickly when he moved to do it again, reaching over and wrapping his arm around his son while putting his hand over the kid's forehead and preventing a second smack to the wood. "Hey," he said gently but firm. "*Stop* it."

The command deflated the boy, who crumpled against his pillow and sobbed. "Everything was perfect and you ruined it. I don't want to live here anymore. I want to be alone. Just leave me alone."

The kid's limbs shook with emotion, and it tore at Matt to see. He patted his back, keeping his hand there briefly before he stood, reluctant to leave. But maybe the kid needed space to calm down and think. "I hope we can get through this, buddy. That you'll be okay."

Brody sniffled but didn't respond, still clutching his blankets as Jessie and Matt moved quietly and closed the door behind them.

Jessie tried to act normal, but the situation wasn't normal and it was impossible to pretend otherwise. Brody's response, although exaggerated, was legitimate and they both knew it. And to prove his point, Brody stayed in his room all day to show he didn't have to accept reality if he didn't want to.

An ability Matt now envied.

He and Jessie spent the evening together, quiet through dinner as they gave Brody time to get his arms around the situation.

The following morning, Matt woke long before dawn, wired and restless about the assignment. He rolled onto his side and curled around Jessie for nearly an hour before finally giving up on sleep and slipping out of bed. He dressed warmly with every intention to take a long walk in the night air to clear his head. But walking down the hallway, he spotted Brody's light glowing under his bedroom door, and he knocked quietly before peering inside to find his son's room empty. The kid's bed looked rumpled but not slept in. His gaze shifted to the nightstand and the untouched dinner plate next to Brody's cell phone. A cold draft blew through the partly open bedroom window, blowing the curtain.

Panic lodged in his throat as logic immediately tried to take over. His son wouldn't run away. Brody still used a nightlight because he hated the dark. It wasn't even sunrise. No way would his child have gone out in the middle of the night.

But where was he? Matt turned and quickly looked

around the rest of the house for any sign of his son. They'd seen him at dinner. He'd refused to eat unless he could take his plate into his room. He'd obviously been crying all day; the boy's eyes had been swollen and red. So they'd both caved and accommodated him. Later, Matt had said goodnight through Brody's bedroom door but the child never responded. Jessie had wanted to check on him but Matt convinced her otherwise. He'd wanted to give his son space. At twelve, a kid needed space. Less hovering.

But his boy wasn't emotionally twelve, was he?

"How could I be so stupid…" Matt muttered, chiding himself as he headed to the master bedroom to wake Jessie. Brody was a bright, autistic child, with the tender feelings and explosive temper of an eight-year-old. What kind of a father wouldn't check on a child like that? How could he have forgotten?

"He's gone," he told Jessie, gently shaking her awake. "Brody's gone."

He'd never seen anyone go from a dead sleep to fully awake so quickly. She threw back the blankets and ducked under his arm, blazing a trail of fire as she ran room to room in nothing but a small nightgown. "Brody! Broooody!"

"Jess, he's not in the house," he said, following her until she tried to run past him and back into Brody's room. He grabbed her shoulders, stopping her. "I checked the entire house before I woke you. He's not here."

She stared up at him, breathing hard as tears welled. Pulling out of his grasp, she quickly stalked down the hallway toward the living room again.

"I was just about to check outside when I woke you," he said, imagining her walking outside in nothing but the nightgown to look for him.

She opened the coat closet and her mouth parted. "He left his coat, Matt." She turned to him, the color draining from her face. "His winter coat is here and he's not. To sneak out, he had to go out his bedroom window without us knowing. We should have checked him, Matt. Now he's gone, and it's freezing out there and he doesn't have his coat. We should have checked him—"

"I know," he said, crossing the space between them and placing his hands on her shoulders. "But you have to stay calm. Look, I'll go search outside while you get dressed. We'll take the vehicles."

She nodded as he spoke, then ran for the master bedroom as he left to check outside the house. He shouted Brody's name, the panic in his voice filtered from the blunt echo that responded. They had no nearby neighbors. No one to have seen him. Matt stared at the dark forest, his blood running cold as the chilly wind blew through his coat. Then he remembered Brody's bike and looked to the side of the house where the boy wasn't supposed to leave it but did anyway. And like Brody, it was gone.

"Still nothing?"

The hollowness of Jessie's voice startled him and he pivoted to see her standing on the porch, dressed in record time and staring at him with what could only be described as the thousand mile stare. He'd seen it before. Her face looked pale and drawn, her eyes swollen and red and searching for direction. She must have read his mind in that instant because she clutched her keys tighter.

"Change of plans," he said, heading for his vehicle. She was in no state of mind to drive, and he didn't dare bring her with him in case... "His bike is gone." He couldn't consider the worst. Not now. Not ever. "Call the ranch. Call Cole McLeod. Call anyone you can think of. But stay here in case he comes back." His heart hammered as he stepped into his SUV and turned the ignition.

She stopped at the screen door and turned to him one last time, a brief glimmer of hope in her eyes before she stepped into the house to make the calls.

He'd read trust in her eyes. Trust in *him*. But why? This was his fault. He should have handled this—all of it— differently. But he'd panicked from the first. Hearing about Jessie's declining health from Terri, then seeing it for himself, had terrified him like nothing ever had. Then when he'd realized Cole McLeod was not only trying to steal Jessie's heart, but Matt's entire life, he'd lost his ability to do anything with his usual control, and he'd been blurting assurances and promises he couldn't possibly keep ever since.

This was on him.

He drove around the property, four or five miles in all directions before heading into town. He received two calls from Jess. One, to tell him that the entire Brewer clan was awake, scattered on horseback and otherwise, looking for their son. The second, to tell him Cole and two other patrol officers were doing the same.

His stomach knotted as he drove through town, around it, and started up the back roads, passing a patrol car. The light of dawn showed him it was McLeod behind the wheel, who gave him a look of concern and a nod. Matt likely looked like hell. He definitely felt like hell. But he acknowledged Cole with a raised hand and drove another mile and a half before the constricted ache in his chest made him pull over and shut off the engine. Surrounded by nothing but trees, he leaned his forehead against the steering wheel, trying to catch his breath. His adrenaline pumped, and without a plan—some kind of direction—he was about to come right out of his skin. He didn't know how to be this person anymore. A husband. A father. He'd been kidding himself. To love this much and have so little control over his loved ones' safety. He couldn't do it. He'd lived most of his life on the edge. Had seen the shocking things people could do to one another. Horrors that chipped away daily at his psyche and trust in humankind.

And never, during any of it, had he felt this horrible and helpless tension-filled panic.

The last few days with Jessie had stripped that other person away, and he desperately needed him back. He thought of his next assignment, focusing on the details as that usual, calculating coldness seeped under his skin. Soon his control had returned and he compartmentalized quickly, burying that growing, splintering panic deep inside before starting the SUV again and heading into the backwoods. Jessie's ringtone eventually sounded and he picked it up before the second ring.

"Tell me he called," he said.

She sniffled. "No, but Luke found him in the stables sleeping in Butterscotch's stall."

He slammed on the brakes in the middle of the dirt road and his eyes welled with tears. "Thank God," he croaked. "Thank. God. Is he okay?"

"He was wearing two sweatshirts but he's cold through and through. Luke said he's a little disoriented but thinks he'll be fine," she said. "Fiona was taking him into the house for a hot bath and a mug of cocoa. I'm calling Cole now to let him know. Do you want me to meet you there?"

He didn't want her driving in her current state. He could barely drive himself. "Stay there. I'll stop by and get you." It was all he could say before he disconnected. Jessie would understand. He wiped his eyes with a hand and finally took a full breath, wondering how often she felt these same emotions when he was off on assignment for months at a time.

How she'd feel as soon as he left her again.

She had to be the strongest woman alive, because in her place, this on a daily basis would have killed him.

*****

Luke met them in the foyer of the main house, smiling and looking relieved. "He's in there," he nodded over his shoulder toward the living room. "Mother said his plan was to stay in the barn until you left, big brother. Then he was going to ask me for a job. He seemed pretty certain you wouldn't be coming back this time and wanted to take care of his mom. Don't be too hard on him. His heart was in the right place."

163

Jessie shook her head. "I'm sorry. We tried talking to him, Luke. Explaining."

Luke grinned again. "Nah, don't worry about it. I ran away once. I didn't make it farther than the barn myself."

"Where is Fiona?" Jessie asked.

"I asked her to give you two time alone with him," he said. "She's in the kitchen with Pop."

Matt patted his brother's shoulder before walking into the living room to find Brody wrapped in a thick blanket and standing by the fire, his back to them as they entered the massive-sized living area, what used to be three separate rooms before his parents took out the walls during a major renovation.

"Hey, kiddo," Matt said.

Brody turned to them, his eyes red.

Matt's heart ached to see him still upset. "Luke said you planned to run away and work on the ranch," he said softly. "I thought we discussed this. You need a high school diploma to work here. You're about six years shy of that."

Brody's lip trembled. "You said you were leaving," he accused.

"I also said I'm coming back. How can your mom and I teach you what you need to graduate," Matt continued, walking slowly toward his son, "if you run off every time there's a miscommunication in this family?"

Brody's face twisted in confusion, eyebrows furrowing. "You're going to teach me, too? You're really coming back for good then? No foolin'?"

"No foolin', sweetie," Jessie said from behind Matt.

"But what if you get hurt?" Brody asked, looking up at his dad. "I heard Mom and Terri talking. What if you die?"

"Don't let your imagination make this more complicated than it is," Matt said. "I'm not hurt. I'm not going to get hurt. And I'm not going to die. I want to be here fulltime to watch you grow up and become a rancher, or a cop or whatever else you decide to be. No one is going to get in the way of me doing that."

Brody's eyes welled with huge tears, his chin quivering as he looked around him. It broke Matt's heart to see his son so overwhelmed and vulnerable. With heavy feet, Brody walked toward his dad, Matt toward his son, and they met in the center of the room as each threw their arms around the other.

Brody sobbed. "I miss you so much when you go," he cried against Matt's chest, finally owning to the emotions he usually projected onto his mother. "I didn't want you to leave again."

"I miss you, too. Just as much," Matt said, brushing back the kid's damp hair and kissing the top of his head. "But you scared me and your mom today. You can't ever leave like that again. We talk things out in this family from now on. Got it?"

"Got it." Brody peered around Matt's arm to look at Jessie. "Sorry, Mom."

"Let's go home," she said. "We have one more day together and I don't want to miss a second of it."

CHAPTER ELEVEN

She opened her eyes to find him already dressed, his bag packed and placed by the bedroom door.

"Matt?" She propped herself on an elbow and looked at the clock, groggy from the early hour and exhausted from their last night together.

"Don't get up," he whispered, crossing the room to where she sat on the bed. "I wanted to get an early start. It'll be easier for Brody not to say goodbye again."

She nodded agreement. Their son had cried half the day yesterday. "So this is it then?" she whispered. "You said you have a meeting first and then you have another flight?"

"Right," he said, sitting next to her.

"Where are you going from there?"

He pulled in a breath and tried for a reassuring smile.

"Sorry," she mumbled. "Not for me to know. I get it." She pushed a hand through her tousled hair. "So this *is* it. The last time we talk until…"

He frowned. "Late March."

"When exactly?"

"I should be stateside again by March 23. I'll call you the second I can."

Stateside. Not just miles away. Another country away. She bit down on her lip, trying not to cry as she nodded.

He enveloped her in his arms. "Promise me you'll take care of yourself," he said, kissing her temple.

"Don't worry about me. And I'll do what I can to keep Brody positive so don't worry about him either."

"Believe it or not, I don't worry about Brody nearly as much as I worry about you. He has *you,*" he said, framing her face with a hand, "and you're a great mother. You on the other hand…you've been looking pale these last few days. You work too many hours and don't get enough sleep."

She didn't want to worry him and pulled back to pinch her cheeks red. "It's just the strain of Brody's wandering off, I think." She patted her cheeks. "See? All better."

"Not exactly the solution I was looking for," he said, the concern obvious in his eyes as he indulged her with a half-grin. "Look at me and tell me you're okay. *Really.*"

She couldn't. She hadn't been well in a long time but she didn't want to tell him that. He needed to stay cool. Focused. Alive. "I'm just not very good at goodbyes," she said, voice quivering.

"This isn't goodbye," he said, pulling her gaze up to his. "It's *see you soon,* remember?"

They'd never said goodbye in the past. Had never said *I love you* like a terrible last farewell in a movie where a main character dies at the end. It was too final. Too much to bear. They acted as though his trips away were trips to the market. Not to Egypt or Afghanistan, or wherever else he was headed this time.

The old familiar knot formed in her throat until her eyes watered. "I guess you'd better go then."

With a frown, he pulled her in his arms again and held her tightly. Pressed a hard kiss against her neck. Then abruptly released her before turning and grabbing his bag.

Through fresh tears, she watched him go. "See you soon," she whispered, listening to the front door close, the

SUV's engine roar to life, and the sound of it as it faded into the distance.

Numb, she turned and stretched out over his side of the bed, the sheets so cold now. She recalled the intensity of their love making last night. Smelled the faint scent of his aftershave on his pillow. Every cell in her body urged her to cry, but she wouldn't allow herself to do that until she held him in her arms again and her tears were tears of joy.

She fell asleep curled against his pillow, and when she woke later from a nightmare, she felt the all-too familiar nausea churn inside, giving her only seconds before she bolted out of bed for the bathroom. She barely made it to the sink before her insides came up. She caught a glimpse of herself as she coughed and heaved while cold perspiration covered her skin, which was paler than paper. When she finally finished, she scooped a handful of water to her mouth before sinking onto the carpet, weak and shaky as her heart pounded an uncomfortable staccato— the first sign of a looming panic attack.

"Not again," she whispered.

*****

She kept herself busy over the next four weeks, pretending. She pretended Matt wasn't away in another country. She pretended her nightmares weren't premonitions of his approaching death. She pretended she wasn't vomiting at all hours of the day or in desperate need of a nap from hour to hour. She pretended not to notice that she was sliding back into her illness without a hope or way out.

Then after a while, pretending became impossible.

She started setting her alarm to wake herself at two in the morning. Forcing food down while half-asleep was the only way to stay somewhat nourished while the remainder of her day she spent spewing anything she ate into a commode. Because with the dawn came clarity, reality, and missing Matt so much that it hurt.

"You should call Dad," Brody said, poking his head into the bathroom Sunday afternoon as she dry-heaved over the master bath sink. "Tell him you're sick. He'll come home."

She pushed a towel over her face. "It was something I ate, sweetie."

"You can't blame it on food when you don't eat, Mom. You're sick again," he said, looming around the doorframe that remained a barrier between them. "You got better when Dad was home and now you're sick again. I hear you in the mornings and sometimes at night. You should go to the doctor."

She already knew her diagnosis. PTSD, and with that came sleeping difficulties, the recurring nightmares featuring Matt in a gruesome death, guilt for letting him go, panic that he wouldn't come back, and the nausea that came with worrying about things for which she had no control.

She ran water into her hand, splashing her face.

"Your hands are shaking."

"That's because I need to eat something, Brody."

"Mom!"

The panic in his voice halted her splashing and she looked up, face dripping as she finally met his gaze in the mirror. "Don't lie to me," he said. "Dad said we wouldn't lie anymore. Why are you sick?"

She couldn't explain. If she could barely understand what was happening to her body, how could she expect a twelve-year-old?

"Call Dad," he said. *"Please."*

A dizzy spell made her reconsider standing and she lowered herself to the floor, inviting him with a pat on the carpet to join her. "Right now, your dad's cell phone is in a locker with his other things," she explained as he sat next to her. "He won't have access to it until he's done with his assignment. That means calling him is pointless. And what would that do to him when he finally gets his messages?

Worry him needlessly, that's what. I'll be fine by the time he finishes this job. And then he'll be home. For good." She held her stomach, staving off another bout of nausea with a gulp of air. "Only two months away. Right?"

"Are you asking me?" He turned to study her. "Because you got sick like this when you guys divorced. When you didn't think he'd come home again. You don't think he's coming back, do you?"

She swallowed several times, trying not to barf as her pulse quickened. "He's coming back, sweetie. But I don't want to talk about it anymore, okay?"

"Why not?"

"Because I feel worse when we do."

"Why? What's wrong with you?"

"I have this…condition, Brody." She leaned forward, pushing her head in her hands as a cold sweat covered her. "It's complicated. Kind of hard to explain."

"Like Asperger's Syndrome?"

She nodded. "A little, but not the same. But I have it, and like you, I need to work my way through it. You know how you have triggers? Things that make it worse?"

"Yeah."

"Well, I have those, too, and talking about your dad being away is a big one. Not because I think he's going to get injured or die but because I miss him. A whole lot. Like the other half of me is missing and I have a big fat hole in my heart. That kind of a lot. Understand?"

"I feel like that sometimes, too."

"I'm sorry, sweetie." She sucked in a breath between numb lips. "I wish this was easier for you."

"Mom? Will you see a doctor anyway? For me?"

She turned to him. "Will it make you feel better if I do?"

"Yes. But I want you to go this week."

She nodded. "Deal. Now stop worrying."

He stared at her. "I'll always worry about you." He shrugged. "You're my mom. Besides, Dad said to take care of you while he's gone. So I'm taking care of you."

She imagined that conversation and smiled. "You do a good job of it." She squeezed his hand and changed the subject. "You know what else makes my condition worse? Bad grades." She crossed her eyes at him, her not-so-subtle sign to let him know she was kidding. "Now let me take care of *you*. Go find a book you want to read and we'll read it together. I could disappear into a good story about now. How about you?"

His smile didn't quite reach his eyes, his doubtful expression reminding her of his father as he pulled himself off the floor to get a book.

*****

She couldn't get in to see her doctor for another two weeks, which was fine with her because she already knew her diagnosis and she was too busy with the deli.

Terri sat on a stool Monday, watching Jessie as she poured her a cup of java. "You look awful."

"Thanks."

"I mean it," Terri said, sipping her coffee. "You look like hammered—"

"Ease up," Jessie said, setting the coffee pot down and wiping her hands on a towel. "I feel, awful, Ter. I don't need to be reminded."

Terri studied her. "Have you heard from him?"

"Of course not."

"Some days I hate men," Terri said, drumming her nails loudly on the glass counter. "Matt specifically. Very much today. Right this instant. He wasn't supposed to do this."

Jessie turned to her. "What's that supposed to mean?"

Her friend's eyes narrowed. "You look pale. When was the last time you ate?"

Jessie avoided the question by seeing to two of her customers' tables. By the time she returned, Terri was giving her the side-eye. "You're not working another twelve-hour shift, are you? Where the hell is Kelley,

171

anyway?"

Jessie took a deep breath and sat on the captain's chair. "Okay, watch this." She opened one of the counter doors and pulled out a scone, taking a bite and tossing it on a plate. "There. Food. I'm eating. See?"

"Yee-haw. We can upgrade you to a whole seventy-eight pounds now."

Jessie put a hand on her hip, trying to chew and not gag. "I will have you know I'm one hundred and ten pounds. For my height, that's still within my weight range. Everyone needs to quit treating me like I have an eating disorder."

Terri sipped her coffee. "Do you have any idea what I'd have to do to get down to a hundred and ten pounds? I'd have to eat a piece of lettuce and maybe one crouton a day for at least a month to get down to that weight. And that's iceberg lettuce, which is like eating water. I don't care what those magazines say, Jessie. One hundred and ten pounds is not healthy. It's a symptom. You look ready to pass out."

"Ter, I love food as much as the next person. But I can't explain it. Stress makes my entire digestive system bail. Asking me to eat this scone right now is like asking me to eat a bar of soap. Everything makes me want to vomit."

"Then don't. Get. Stressed," Terri said. "Look, he can handle himself. I mean, I trust him. What does that tell you?"

"You don't trust men at all," Jessie said. "Who are you kidding?"

"I do, too." Her eyebrows arched. "In fact, if it was the end of the world with zombies everywhere, I'd want you and Matt with me. Want to know why?"

"Because you need to quit binge-watching that show so I don't have to pretend for two seconds that we're actually considering what we'd do during a zombie apocalypse."

"That's not it at all," Terri said with a dismissing wave.

"I'd want you both with me because you're my best friend, and if I'm with you, he's not going to let anything happen to me either. He's a survivor, Jessie. Now I mean it. Quit worrying."

The mere subject of Matt made her throat close, but she tried taking another bite of the soap scone anyway to make Terri happy. She worked past her gag reflex and swallowed, then took another bite. Her body felt hot all over and she took a sip of water before pushing the plate toward Terri. "You finish it."

Jessie's sister, Kelley, walked in for her shift then, bringing in the entire southern cold snap with her as she held the door open too long while shaking the sleet off her coat.

"'Bout time, little sister," Terri said, who loved playing the disapproving older sister with Jessie.

"Any word from Matt?" Kelley said, ignoring Terri's taunt as she pulled a hand through her dark hair to shake off more sleet.

Jessie stood to glare at Kelley. "You both are making me gray, you know that? Eight more weeks. How many updates do you need? Last week it was nine weeks. Next week I'll tell you seven. Then six. Then five. Why do I have to keep repeating myself?" A third customer flagged her for a refill and she grabbed the decaf pot. "Everyone keeps asking me about him. Matt, Matt, Matt," she said, rounding the counter corner as the cold air hit her in a single wave. "Is it any wonder I'm—" She fell back a step when dizziness combined with crippling nausea knocked her backward like a one-two punch.

Kelley halted all movement by the coat rack. "Jessie? What's wrong with you?"

Jessie wavered, opening her mouth to respond when the shop's lights dimmed. She looked to Terri, her heart pounding as the image of her friend briefly framed to black.

"Jessie…" Terri slipped off her stool. "Jessie!"

Terri and Kelley's following shouts sounded distant as they rushed toward her. She wanted to tell anyone who would listen that she was all right, but her mouth wouldn't form the words. Then her knees buckled and she started to fall.

*****

She opened her eyes to find herself staring at a ceiling she didn't recognize. Sterile shouldn't have a smell, but it did, and she figured out with one inhale that she was in a hospital room. She shifted on the bed, dry-mouthed as she turned to see Terri sitting by her bedside.

"What happened?" she croaked.

"You don't remember?" Terri let go of Jessie's hand and wiped her red eyes. "You passed out, you big dope."

She blinked, unable to recall much of anything. "I did?" She had an image of Kelley's pretty face staring down at her. "I don't remember. Was Kelley there?"

"Yes, she was. And let me tell you," Terri said, grabbing a Kleenex and blowing her nose, "that I am officially going to stop being your friend if you ever do that again. I practically had a heart attack. But do you care about my wellbeing? No."

Jessie felt something cold in her arm and realized she had an IV tube attached to her. Her other hand was wrapped in a bandage. "What happened to my hand?"

"The coffee. It splashed and burned you when you fell."

"Bad?"

"Bad *enough.*"

Jessie licked her dry lips and tried moving, the soreness in her limbs lifting the fog a little. "Wait." She twisted to sit up. "Where's Brody? And the store. What time is it?"

Terri put her hand on her shoulder and forced her back down. "Settle down. Kelley has the shop under control so that you'll stay put, and Brody is fine. I called Matt's parents when I found out the doctors planned to keep you here overnight. Possibly longer if you keep trying to get up."

She tried getting up anyway. *"Overnight?* Um, no."

Terri held her against the pillows again. "We'll keep doing this dance if you insist on getting up. Now stay down. Don't make me karate chop you into submission. The doctor said you need to relax and quit getting yourself excited. So stop getting yourself excited. We're handling everything, okay?"

"But Brody—"

"Luke stopped by your house to get Brody, and Fiona assured me they'll keep him as long as you need. She said he has clothes at the ranch and that you're not to worry about a single thing. And once Brody's settled in, Luke and Tessa are coming to check on you. Fiona and Stern plan to drop by later tonight. They're trying for a little subtlety. We don't want the entire Brewer brood leaving the ranch and getting Brody all stirred up."

"Don't let them bring him here. Please," she said, swallowing past her dry throat. "Brody would see the monitors and have a total freak out."

"We won't." Terri shook her head. "We're all aware how much that kid loves his parents. And he worries about you like a mother hen. Seeing you here would be much too upsetting. We know that."

"He knows I'm sick, Ter. It's been too difficult to hide lately and he called me out on it Sunday. But he doesn't know *what's* wrong, and I have no idea how to explain PTSD to a twelve-year-old."

"Luke said Brody thinks you're here because you promised him you'd see a doctor this week. He's really quite calm about the whole thing. Thinks this was the plan all along."

"Good. Well, tell him I'll be home tomorrow."

"But you don't know that."

"Never mind," Jessie said. "I'll tell him myself when I call him later."

Terri rolled her eyes.

The doctor entered her room then, affording her a brief smile before looking at her chart. "Ms. Brewer. Glad you're awake again."

"Awake again?"

"You woke earlier," Terri said. "You really don't remember? You spoke to the doc and everything. He flashed a light in your eyes. How could you not remember that?"

Jessie frowned, unable to recall. "What'd I say?"

"Something about getting more coffee for table number four," Terri said. "You should probably try to get out of the deli more often."

Jessie sighed.

"We have a few things to discuss," the doctor said, looking at Terri, who returned his stare for a long moment before jumping out of her seat.

"Ah. Gotcha." She grabbed her purse and turned to Jessie. "I'll be right outside, hon."

The doctor introduced himself, standing next to her bed as he explained the details of her low blood pressure and high pulse rate due to severe dehydration. Explained how she was to stay in the hospital overnight, possibly longer, until they were positive the baby's health wasn't at risk.

"Wait, what? *Baby?* I'm…pregnant?"

"That's correct." He looked at her doubtfully. "You weren't aware?"

She shook her head. "You're really sure?"

He smiled and clasped his hands together, rocking back on his heels. "Positive."

"I couldn't be far along." She pressed her hand to her abdomen. "You're absolutely certain?"

"You're profoundly pregnant, Ms. Brewer."

"Really?" Her eyes widened. "What is *profoundly* pregnant? What is that…twins? Triplets? Holy—"

He chuckled. "No, it's this old doctor's way of saying we're certain you're pregnant. However, if you require another test, we can certainly—"

"No." The first night with Matt came rushing back. Then the second. Third. And every night after. "No test necessary. It's possible. *Very* possible. I'm—I'm just in a bit of a shock right now." She put fingers over her mouth as nausea bubbled up. "Um, do you have something safe I can take for nausea? Or a bucket? Because I'm about to be sick." She pushed her fingers over her mouth. *"Soon."*

His eyebrows lifted and he quickly handed her a small tin large enough to hold a cup of water before shuffling out of the room. She blinked, staring at the absurdity of it when a nurse quickly followed him back. Jessie turned on her side to face them, which made the nausea a little better as the nurse produced a bigger barf pan, just in case.

"If I have any visitors," Jessie told the doctor while the nurse adjusted her IV and produced a pill for her to take, "I'd like this news to stay between us for now."

"Of course," the doctor said. "Is there a father present?"

Present? "Not at the moment," she murmured, sliding her hand over her abdomen again. "But there will be. In eight weeks." She prayed she was right about that.

Tessa and Luke showed up shortly after the doctor left. Luke explained Terri's absence. That she'd gone home to change clothes and would be back within the hour. He gave Jessie a hug for Brody as Tessa rearranged the plate of food—Jessie's *dinner*—that the nurse had placed in front of her while they talked about the festival's success. Jessie nibbled at a dry piece of bread as Luke made her laugh with comical stories of his time in the hospital and physical rehabilitation.

Terri returned and kept her company until Stern and Fiona stopped by to give her an update on Brody. Fiona even offered to help him with American Literature during his impromptu break from homeschool and Jessie happily agreed.

After everyone left at seven-thirty, Jessie called Brody

on his cell phone, listening to the details of his day, and how much he'd missed her and could they please adopt a cat. Hearing his voice calmed her nerves. He sounded happy and healthy. He'd be fine with the Brewers. She had no doubt of it.

She fell asleep sometime after the call, waking several hours later from yet another nightmare that left her clutching her throat and unable to breathe. Without the comforts of home and only a small overhead light above her bed, it took a while for her to talk herself down from the panic. Thankfully, the medication for the nausea had worked. It was the first time in weeks she hadn't woken and immediately rushed to the bathroom to throw up her guts. She adjusted the bed until she sat upright, listening to the quiet of the hospital then until her thoughts settled and anchored.

She turned to her cell that Terri had left on her bedside table with the demand to call her if she needed anything at all. Moving the IV drip out of her way, she picked up the phone and dialed Matt.

His voice, warm and strong, greeted her, and tears streamed down her face as she listened to the brief message. The tone sounded, waiting for her.

"Hey, it's me," she finally said, giggling as she suddenly became self-conscious. "Gosh, I think this is the first time I've called you while you were on assignment. I don't know how long I have on this thing before it cuts me off. But Matt…there's something you should know."

CHAPTER TWELVE

Matt dragged himself into the hotel room and tossed his bag on the bed, his bones tired, his muscles sore, and his mind ready for sleep. He was finally done with this part of his life, and he doubted he'd ever miss it. He hadn't realized just how much that was true until he'd touched down in the states again. His first thought had flown to his family. Violet Valley. The ranch. Home.

He knew he should give himself the usual two or three days before calling Jessie. A period of adjustment to get back in touch with civilian life so he wouldn't sound like the disconnected stranger—the identity they'd created for him—that he'd become during his time away. He always tried to spare her that…awkwardness, and in truth, he didn't want her to see that side of him. But it was more difficult this time because he desperately needed to hear her voice. To know she was still home, waiting for him.

He dug into his bag and pulled out the phone he hadn't looked at in three months. He hooked up the thing to its charger before stepping into a shower, where he disappeared under the hot spray until it ran cool.

Forty minutes later, he sat on the hotel chair, his hair still damp when he checked his messages. Twenty-one messages, to be exact, which was absurd. Something big had to have happened at home. Like the whole of Violet Valley burned down.

He pulled in a steadying breath and leaned forward, resting his elbows on his knees as he checked the first message.

"This is Max. Have another job when you get back. Call me."

The man was relentless. He skipped to the second message.

"Hi, Dad. Mom is sick and she won't call you." Matt clenched the phone. "She said you won't get this message but I'm calling anyway. You should come home now. I miss you. Mom misses you. She says she misses you like a big hole is in her heart. That's probably why she keeps throwing up. Okay. So, come back soon. And don't get hurt. Okay, love you. Bye."

Frowning, he stared at the phone, his heart pounding. Jessie sounded worse. Much worse. He clicked over to the third message.

"Heeeello. This is Terri. Probably didn't expect to hear from me, did ya? I want to say right off that this was *so* not part of our agreement." Silence. "Right. We didn't really *have* an agreement. I get that. But we were working together. Similar agendas and everything. But then you left again and I realize now that you must be an idiot. So let me spell out a few things. Jessie needs you. Brody needs you. And you better get your butt back here in one piece as soon as possible. My best friend is sick as a dog and I blame you for that. *Sick.* Get me? *As a dog!* Okay then. I'm done with my rant. Get home soon. And take care. And…I just love you guys so much." She sobbed. "Get home. Okay. Bye."

He ran a hand down his face. A call from Terri—a sobbing Terri, no less—was proof that Jessie's health had deteriorated to a scary level when he left. Screw this. He was finding a red-eye and leaving tonight. He skipped to the fourth message.

"Hey, it's me." His shoulders sagged when her sweet voice drifted through him, what felt like a fresh summer breeze blowing into the cold hotel room. "Gosh, I think this is the first time—" He rubbed the back of his neck as he listened to her voice, eyes watering. This trip had been the worst. He hadn't been able to compartmentalize and do the job. He'd missed her. As in, *never-seeing-the-sky-again* missed her. Hearing her voice now with no immediate way to hold her was almost more than he could bear.

"But Matt…there's something you should know," she said, sniffling into the phone. "I guess I'm *profoundly* pregnant, whatever that means." Quickly slack-jawed, he jammed a hand into his damp hair and clutched his phone tighter. "It doesn't mean *anything*, actually. The doctor was trying to be funny. But I *am* pregnant. That much is true." Long pause. "Sorry, I'm still getting used to it. So I've been thinking about that first night…when you said you hoped we were pregnant? I realize it could have been the moment talking, because we'd taken yet another step in a different direction than we'd planned, but I hope you meant it. That you want a baby. Because it looks like that's what we're doing. Sorry, I'm rambling. This is all so new." She sighed, sounding overwhelmed. "I guess what I'm trying to say is that I know you won't get this message for another eight weeks, but I wanted to be the first to tell you. I wanted you to be the first to hear this because you should be here and you're not." He heard tears in her voice. "Not that I'm blaming you or anything. I just wish you were here to tell. And you're not. And by the time you get back, Terri will know because she's hovering like you wouldn't believe and I need to tell her something to make her feel better. Of course that means half the town will probably know, too. But I wanted you to be the first. Technically, you're the first person I've told. You're going to be a daddy again, Matt. And—" She sniffled. "Okay, I have to quit crying. I'm working myself up and the doctor told me no more working myself up. I'm happy, Matt. I'm just so happy. I wish you were here to tell in person. Okay, let me change the subject before I get ridiculous. Brody is doing okay. He *loves* the hippotherapy. He's taking care of me like you asked. He misses you as much as—"

The message cut her off and he stared at his phone. Forwarded to the next voicemail.

"Me again," she said. "I do hate these things. Remind me to crush your phone when you get home." She cried. Then giggled. "It's night here but I'm awake enough to realize how silly I sound. Probably because I'm so happy. And emotional. That's pregnant for you. I have my hand on my belly right now. Where he or she is growing." He could hear her smile over the phone and more tears formed. "I'm hoping we have a little girl. Not because I don't want another boy. I do. I want another boy, too. But this time I'd like—I imagine you with a little girl and—" She sniffled, voice shaking. "I'm being crazy, aren't I? Rambling as usual. This is why I don't leave messages. But if we have a girl, I was thinking maybe Molly. Do you like Molly? But if we have a boy, maybe Aaron? I'm kind of loving every name right now. You're going to have to help me narrow it down. Sorry, I'm babbling. I found out only a few hours ago and I couldn't wait—"

The message cut her off. He wiped his eyes, crying now. He could count on one hand all the times he'd cried his entire life. Pulling in a breath, he skipped to the next message.

She sighed, her voice suddenly serious when she spoke. "The baby isn't the only reason I called you, Matt. I wanted to tell you…no, I *needed* to tell you something that I should have said a long time ago. It can't wait. I just…I know you take responsibility for us. Brody and I. In your heart. And that's okay. I do the same. But the last two weeks you were here, you blamed yourself for all that happened. It was clear on your face. Brody running off. My health—oh, gosh—one more thing we haven't talked about. You were right, Matt. When you suggested that I'm sick. I've been sick for a while. A few years. But like Brody's issues, I kept it from you. I thought I was protecting you but it all seems so stupid now. It would seem I let the stress of Brody's issues and worrying about this insane profession of yours get to me. It wasn't your fault and I didn't want you to think it was. But you weren't here and Brody needed me and I was getting too sick to keep up with his needs. Something had to give. That's why the divorce, Matt. It wasn't the fighting. I thought if I cut you out completely, I'd stop worrying about you. That I'd stop waking up scared and going to bed sick with worry. But after you moved out, after we cut off communication, I—" she let out a shaky breath, "well, things got worse." He covered his mouth, his heart breaking to hear the tears in her voice. "I never realized how much I counted on hearing your voice all the time. And then you were gone and things…my health spiraled. But I don't want to talk about that. It no longer matters. Because when I look back now, through all of it, I think our hearts were in the right place, don't you? We were just trying to take care of each other in our own way and—"

Another cut off. He skipped to the next message, covering his eyes as tears streamed down his face.

She inhaled and let out another shaky breath. "My point is that…maybe you haven't always given me what I needed, but you always gave me what you had. You gave me *everything* you had, Matt, and I know that. I didn't say the words when you were here, and you didn't, I guess because we've always played these stupid little games so we wouldn't tempt fate. But I wanted to say it aloud again, to tell you how much I love you. Because I do. I've always loved you. Even when we weren't together I loved you." She sobbed. "Okay, I'm ramping myself up again. This will be my last call because I'm supposed to stay calm and I can never stay calm when I think about you out there. Away from me. So very far away." She muffled another sob. "So this is it," she whispered, pausing with another sniffle. "See you soon."

The call disconnected and he dropped his phone on the floor, pushing his face into his hands. For several minutes, he couldn't stop the tears that rolled down his face, and when he finally managed to pull it together, he grabbed his laptop and checked for redeye flights from D.C. to Atlanta, finding none.

He called Max, who answered on the third ring.

"Matt," he said gruffly. "What the hell? Do you know what time it is?"

"I do. And I need a plane. Now. It's urgent."

"A plane?"

"Right."

"But it's the middle of the night."

"Yeah, and I believe you owe me a number of I-owe-you-big favors. I'm cashing them all in. Get me a plane to Atlanta. I don't care if it's a cargo plane. Just get me on it. I'm needed at home."

*****

It was still early when he pulled into the drive with daylight only a couple hours away. He was tired, in serious need of decompression, but most of all, he desperately needed to see Jessie again.

He let himself in through the front door, quiet so he wouldn't wake anyone, when he noticed the kitchen light on and a shadowy figure looming. Jessie poked her head around the corner, looking squinty-eyed and half-asleep.

"Hello?" she said, chewing something juicy and holding what looked like a piece of orange.

"Jess," he whispered. "What are you doing up at this hour?"

Her eyes widened. She swallowed and dropped the half slice of orange to the floor. "Matt!" He released his bag as she crossed the space between them in five quick hops and jumped into his arms, wearing nothing more than one of his shirts and bikini underwear as she straddled his waist.

"You're early!" She squealed, wiggling her feet and hugging him tightly as she kissed him hard on the neck. "This is so great! Oh, I missed you!"

He closed his eyes as she hugged him, a mountain of tension draining from his shoulders just to hold her again. "You don't know," he said, hugging her tighter. "How much. I've missed you. Both of you." He pulled back. "Is Brody okay?"

She smiled so brightly that his chest ached to see it. "He had a special hippotherapy thing in the morning and stayed at your parent's tonight." She wiggled her eyebrows suggestively. "We have the place to ourselves."

He kissed her then, long and demanding as he pressed her against the wall while she adjusted her legs around his waist. She smelled so good that he couldn't help himself as he lowered his head and kissed her neck, his hands gripping her thighs tighter, thinking of little else than the smoothness of her skin. "You should be resting, shouldn't you? The baby? Your condition? Are you okay?"

"I'm fine." She kissed him again. "More than fine. Perfectly fine. Let's talk later," she whispered, her next kiss demanding that he kiss her back as she pushed her fingers through his longer hair.

"You're sure?" he whispered between kisses. She nodded eagerly as he carried her to the back room and lowered her to the soft bed. She pulled off his shirt as he unbuttoned hers, followed by more hurried movements until their clothes were off and he was sliding under the covers with her.

Making love with Jessie after a long assignment had always been fast and intense. He lost himself instantly and completely, deep inside her, as she dug her fingers into his shoulders and closed her eyes. He watched her bite her lip. Heard the change in her moans with each thrust. Felt the familiar arch in her back as her calves slid behind his thighs, pulling him deeper and deeper, until that sound of ecstasy escaped her lips. He came the second she did, moaning and holding her tightly as he slipped over that edge of control with her.

They barely moved, just breathing as they waited for reality to sink in. Waiting for the reality to begin where he wouldn't have to leave his family for months at a time. He wanted to see Jessie healthy again. He wanted to see her happy, immensely happy as she'd been over the phone. As she was now in his arms. He had every intention to keep her happy every day for the rest of their lives.

When he finally moved, he raised his head to watch her slowly come back to him with a small smile and giggle. Her smile turned shy as she looked up at him and pushed his damp hair back from his forehead. "How did you get here so early?"

He arched an eyebrow and grinned. "Wow, really? Complaints?"

"Not at all." She giggled again. "I was hoping for a phone call tonight. Look what I got instead."

He almost laughed at her satisfied smirk. "I got your message. Or should I say messages. After that, nothing was going to keep me away from you tonight."

She searched his face, that familiar worry in her eyes. "No downtime though. Are you okay?"

She knew the drill. Knew that he spent days, sometimes weeks, reorienting himself back to the reality that was Violet Valley, regular life, and family. "I will be. Just being here with you helps. Seeing you. I had to see you."

"I'm glad you couldn't wait." She wiggled underneath him, looking supremely satisfied.. "Obviously."

He smiled and took care as he lifted himself off her and shifted his body until they were facing each other, buried under the blankets. He ran his hand softly down her arm, her hip, resting it on her waist. He couldn't stop touching her. Never wanted to be parted from her again.

Her eyes searched his face, worried. Always worried.

"So it sounds like I need to make an honest woman out of you," he said with a smile, brushing her cheek with his thumb.

She let out a soft laugh and pressed her fingertips against the scruff of an early-morning beard he hadn't bothered to shave earlier. "Are you happy about the baby, too?" she whispered. "Please say yes."

"Are you kidding?" He'd been so happy he'd cried like a baby in his hotel room for several minutes, but he wasn't about to tell her that. "Of course I am. I love this child's mother more than anything. I'm beyond happy. I'm over the damn moon, Jess." He ran his hand over her hip again, her waist, resting the tips of his fingers against her flat abdomen that wasn't yet showing. "I told you I wanted to get you pregnant that night. I meant it."

"I think that's when it happened," she said, her pallor from weeks ago replaced now with a glowing smile. "By the doctor's calculations, anyway."

"You wear pregnancy well," he said, stroking her cheek. "You're radiant, Jess. I was terrified of how I'd find you. Your health. Between the other voicemails—"

"*Other* voicemails?"

"I didn't mention those?" She shook her head as he adjusted his arm under his pillow. "I had about ten voicemails behind yours from practically every member of my family, giving me updates about your hospital stay. Three from Terri. Even Kelley left one."

"Kelley? You're kidding."

He shook his head. "She wanted to assure me she'd stepped it up at the deli. That you wouldn't be working full days anymore. Your hospital stay really scared her."

"She's been so faithful since it happened. The poor thing. I'm such a mean old sister for getting sick and putting a halt to her wild ways. I'm sure she'll make up for lost time later."

He brushed his hand along her arm. "You never mentioned it in your messages. That you were at the hospital. Were you planning to tell me?"

She paused, her eyes searching his. "No."

Her honesty surprised him. "Why?"

She shrugged. "Because I'd be out of the hospital by the time you received the message. There was no point to worry you when the urgency of the situation would no longer matter. Was Kelley the only one who let the cat out of the bag?"

"No, just about everyone clued me in. You should know by now that you can't be a Violet Valley resident without everyone getting into your business. Still, I should have heard that news from you, Jess."

"I blame the baby," she said. "I was giddy to tell you about her. Or him. And I needed to tell you those other things, too. That I love you. That I don't blame you for my health spiral. All of it. It couldn't wait."

He leaned over and brushed his lips against hers.

"I was at the hospital when I called you," she said when he pulled back from the kiss. "It honestly never occurred to me to mention it. And then afterward there was no point. Don't be mad."

"I'm not mad. But I hope you meant everything you said. That you're going to start letting me in."

"I let you in," she said.

"Sometimes. When it suits you. But there is such a thing as being too independent, Jess. I know that taking care of your dad and raising your sister had a lot to do with that, but those years are over. Now you have me. And we're both Brody's parents. You can trust me to handle half the strain. Maybe more. If you need me. And the baby—I missed half of Brody's childhood. I want to be here with this baby. I want to be here for everything."

She smiled. "You may regret that offer. This baby is keeping me up all night."

"I thought you were feeling better."

"I am. In fact, it's the opposite now. I can't stop eating. This baby is constantly hungry at night. I'm craving citrus. Anything citrus." She paused, thinking. "Wait, I totally dropped an orange on the floor back there, didn't I?"

"Forget it. It'll be there in the morning."

"Yeah." She wrinkled her nose. "With ants."

He laughed. "Wrong season."

"You're right. Still. Yuck."

He didn't want her leaving his side and quickly covered her hand with his, threading his fingers through hers. "Any *other* cravings?"

She sighed a sound of pure happiness. "Eggs. Any kind of eggs." Her eyes widened. "Oh, and bacon." He grinned and she pressed her finger against his chest, suddenly serious. "I've gained ten pounds in eight weeks. I'm afraid this is a forewarning that midnight feedings might be a nightmare. Are you up for that?"

"I'm up for anything."

"Really? Even a cat?"

"A cat?"

"Brody wants a cat."

He smiled. "Okay. A cat. We'll pick up Brody first thing tomorrow after the therapy training and stop by the shelter for a cat. I'm up for all of it." He brushed his hand against her belly, picturing her healthy and round with their child—everything he'd missed with Brody. He imagined his family growing. Kids everywhere. Exactly as they'd planned before things went sideways. "But you have to talk to me…tell me when I need to step it up or whatever. It terrified me hearing those messages about you, Jess. First Brody. Then Terri. Luke and Tessa. Even my mother called to tell me you'd passed out at the deli. She said you burned your hand with coffee. The woman was completely unhinged."

"Matt, don't take this wrong, but your mother is always unhinged."

He chuckled. "True, but you have to promise me. *No more.* No more missed meals. No more passing out. No more secrets. Tell me how you're feeling."

She nodded and pulled his hand to her lips, kissing his knuckle. "I promise. But you have to promise the same.

You need to talk to me, too."

"I talk to you." He sat up on his elbow. "We're talking right now."

"I mean confide in me. When it's important. When you *really* need to. When you don't want to." She paused, brushing her fingers over his hand repeatedly. "When *your* nightmares start again. No more secrets like before. No more trying to protect me from what you do—or have done—in the past. The bad dreams. The cold sweats. I'm not oblivious, you know. You need to talk to me if they start. Promise you will?"

He swallowed. Knew it wouldn't be easy. But he couldn't ask of her what he wasn't willing to do himself. "No more secrets," he said, kissing her forehead. "I promise."

"Promise me something else?"

"What?"

She paused, suddenly looking shy. "Marry me?" Her eyes watered, shining brightly. "Again? Soon? Next weekend if possible?"

He looked down at her fingers brushing over his, noticing for the first time her wedding ring.

"I put it on again," she whispered. "Right after the hospital. After I learned about the baby. Is that okay?"

He'd promised himself he wouldn't get misty-eyed again tonight, but seeing that ring nearly pushed him over the edge. "I'll marry you tomorrow if you want," he said, kissing her quickly so she couldn't see. "Wherever. Whenever. But we don't have to rush if you want to plan something with family and friends. It doesn't matter to me when. I've never truly felt like you weren't mine, Jess. In my heart. Even since the divorce. You'll always be mine."

"I feel that way, too." She brushed her hand over his chest. His arm. His face. "I still can't believe you're finally here. It doesn't feel real."

He kissed her temple. "It never does for me, at least for the first week or two." Letting go of a weary sigh, he shifted onto his back, placing a hand behind his head before pulling her against him as he tried to shut out all that he'd left behind. A life he no longer wanted.

She snuggled against his side. "Are you okay? You swear?"

"I'm…better," he said, holding her tight against him. "It'll take a while but I'll get there." He turned to those beautiful eyes shining up at him. "Somehow you bring me back, Jess. Every time. It's not overnight, but you always bring me back."

"And this time," she whispered, settling in comfortably, "you're back for good. Here with us and home to stay."

Home to stay. The fatigue slowly drained from his body as those three words resonated in his brain. When Jessie's grip relaxed and her breathing leveled into a pattern against his chest, he knew she'd fallen asleep and finally closed his eyes to join her. Settled. Happy.

Home to stay.

ABOUT THE AUTHOR

Callie spent the first three decades of her life in Portland, Oregon before picking up everything and moving to the South for much needed sunshine and a change of pace.

When she's not reading or penning contemporary romance and young adult novels, she's absorbed in all things supernatural, fantasy, sci-fi, anime, and of course, romance. She's also very devoted to her numerous adopted animals.

Discover other titles by Callie James:
https://calliejamesauthor.com

Please connect with me online:

Twitter: https://twitter.com/CallieJames
Facebook: https://www.facebook.com/CallieJames
Goodreads: https://www.goodreads.com/CallieJames

CPSIA information can be obtained at www.ICGtesting.com
Printed in the USA
BVOW08s1426231016

465802BV00001B/108/P

9 780990 364634